Introduction:

This is the second edition of *To Find What was Lost* which was the first in a multibook series featuring the small northwestern Michigan town of Manitou. The same character are involved in each of the series although their importance to the story varies with each book. They also age throughout the stories much the same as we age. Babies are born, divorces happen, people die and newcomers arrive with their own story.

The stories are based on everyday situation and current events. Subject matter includes starting over, homelessness, runaways, the treatment of veterans, environmental issues, mafia and housing.

There is a good mixture of mystery, intricate plots and romance but at the end the reader will be left feeling good. I hope you enjoy all the books in the series as well as other books I have written.

James H. Goodwin
2018

To Find What Was Lost

Prologue

It's strange that she had something else on her mind while trying to unbuckle her three-year-old son from his car seat before the flaming oil reached the car. For a fraction of a second she was preoccupied with thoughts about the argument that led to this deadly situation.

Only minutes before Shelly had glared at her husband with fire in her eyes and said "For Christ's sake, it's your mother, Drew. Why am I the only one worrying about her birthday gift?"

He turned from the desk where he was working on 2nd quarter financials and looked at his wife. "I told you I'd get something tomorrow. I need to finish the financial work to make sure there's money to feed and clothe our family."

Shelly threw up her arms in disgust and said, "Forget it. Tomorrow will be too late. She's coming to our house for dinner, and she'll be expecting something. Damn it, I'll take Bobby and go right now before it gets too late."

Bobby, their three-year-old, was playing with his Minion characters on the living room floor and whined when his mother took him away from his play. It was a very cold early spring day in Gloucester, and the northeast wind blowing off the ocean made it feel more like winter. Shelly put a coat and hat on Bobby and grabbed her own coat and purse and was out the door. She was still ticked off at Drew and didn't even acknowledge him when he cautioned her to drive carefully. In fact, his warning to drive carefully made her even angrier, and she slammed the car into reverse, spitting gravel as she backed out the driveway.

Their house was on Harrison Avenue, which was a long steep hill that crossed busy Eastern Avenue, the primary road to Rockport. As a result, there was heavy traffic on Eastern Avenue year-round. Shelly threw the car into drive and headed down the hill. The weather had turned nasty, and an icy rain was making the road slick and even her windshield wipers were useless. She was most likely going a little too fast, because when she stepped on the brakes at the bottom of the hill, the car continued to slide through the stop sign and into the middle of Eastern Avenue. In her rush to move the car, she somehow managed to stall it.

Shelly saw the tank truck coming towards her and observed the panic on the driver's face as he slammed on his brakes. The freezing rain combined with the speed of the truck resulted in the truck sliding while the tanker section jackknifed. He tried to stop, but to no avail. The semi-tractor hit the old style granite curb stones with such force that it flipped over, followed by the flipping of the tanker. Everything seemed to be in slow motion as the semi and tanker slid on their sides, leaving a trail of sparks and flowing oil. Shelly was petrified but breathed a sigh of relief when it looked as if the truck wasn't going to reach her vehicle.

She unbuckled her seat belt and scrambled to the back door of her car. Just as she was opening the door everything changed. The sky lit up like daylight from the burning fuel oil leaking from the tanker, and the heat from the fire felt like a pizza oven. She worked fast to get Bobby out of his car seat, all the while watching the flaming oil running down the street toward her. The last thing she heard as the flames overtook her was Drew yelling her name. It was over quickly for Shelly and Bobby. The intense heat and flames kept anyone foolish enough to try to rescue them from getting close to the car.

Drew heard the crash of the truck and ran down the hill fearing that Shelly had been in an accident. What he witnessed was something no one should have to see. Just as he arrived at the corner his wife was opening the back door trying to get to their son when their whole car became engulfed in flaming oil. He knew then, at that time and place, his life would forever be changed.

Shelly was a popular real estate agent in Gloucester. Her face was familiar to thousands of residents who saw it plastered on the ad panels attached to the sides of buses and in weekly flyers. She had many acquaintances on the island community, but Drew was more amazed at the number of friends she had made since they moved back to his hometown 5 years ago. None of that mattered now because she was gone. He was so distraught that he was in no shape to contribute to funeral plans and left that to his mother and in-laws which they willingly but sadly accepted. When he later learned that Shelly's parents had played a big part in the funeral plans, he could barely face them due to his feelings of guilt.

Drew and Shelly didn't belong to a church, but his mother was an active member of the Unitarian Universalist Church so it seemed logical to hold the service there. It's Gloucester's oldest church building in continuous operation since being built in 1806. It's the home of America's first Universalist Society and their lantern steeple has guided generations of mariners into port. Drew's mother thought maybe the steeple will lead him to some level of peace and comfort. It also has one of the largest seating capacities in the city, and on the day of the funeral almost all of the seats were taken. He personally didn't remember a thing about that day, but his mother reported that it was a beautiful service.

The next couple of months passed without Drew really comprehending much of what was going on. His mother handled most of the day to day things in his life except for certain business details which needed his attention. Drew owned and operated two car washes in town and in case someone thinks it's a simple business they should think again. There're many things that can go wrong- from mechanical failures to staffing problems. When everything's running smoothly the businesses are like the magical money tree but when there are problems they are like the black hole that sucks money out of the air. A seaside town like Gloucester has to constantly fight the ravage of the salt air, and for that reason many people choose to wash their cars often. However, salt's also the very reason the car wash equipment fails so frequently.

A couple of months after the loss of his wife and child, it was pretty clear that Drew had lost the heart to run a business and if he didn't do something quickly there would be no business to sell. His mother was a huge support to him, and although he knew she too was grieving the loss of her only grandchild she managed to keep him somewhat focused. When he told her his plan to sell the car washes she was totally supportive. He then was completely surprised by how quickly the businesses sold. Four months after Shelly's death he was a man out of work who was still mourning the loss of his wife and son.

Drew's lifelong friends tried their best to bring him out of his funk, but eventually they gave up. He spent most days watching reruns of game shows on TV, and as long as it was light and funny he could handle it. Once the news came on, he had to turn the TV off. Thankfully, he never developed the desire for alcohol, or he'd have been drunk all the time. About seven months after the deaths he received a call from the attorney his mother hired to deal with the accident. He really didn't care to deal with the issue as he wasn't looking for someone to blame in the accident because he blamed himself.

The attorney asked Drew if he'd meet with him at his office because there was a notary there if they needed one. His office was easy to find because it was on Main Street and not far from the old North Shore Theater where he went as a child with friends on Saturday afternoons to see a movie. The meeting with the attorney took only fifteen minutes and ended when Drew was presented with a check for three and a half million dollars. This was his portion of the settlement from the tanker company after the attorney took his fee. The money made Drew feel sick and only exacerbated his feelings of guilt. All he could think was that now he had the money to do whatever he wanted and all Drew wanted was to have his wife and son back.

Chapter One

Five Months Later

It's been a year since the accident and Drew wasn't functioning much better than he had the first couple of months. Friends and neighbors were no longer calling to check up on him because all he did was bum them out. With the money he made by selling the car washes and the settlement from the accident, he really didn't have to work again. In fact he'd developed the attitude that he didn't have to do anything again including his laundry, cooking, cleaning house or even bathing.

One afternoon while Drew was lying on the couch the doorbell rang. When he didn't answer, the person proceeded to knock hard on the window. He finally had enough of the annoyance and opening the door, was surprised to see Shelly's mother standing there alone. Before Drew could even speak she told him to hush and began eyeing him up and down. He had always liked Nancy and felt as if he had a great relationship with his mother-in-law. Still, he hesitantly said, "I'm really surprised to see you. Would you like to come in?" Once she stepped to the foyer he asked what she was doing in this part of the country. Shelly had been raised in Northern Michigan in a little town on the shore of Lake Michigan, but her parents had relocated to Dallas after her senior year in high school when her father was transferred to another paper mill.

Nancy said, "I came here to see you. Your mother and I've been talking on a regular basis and needless to say she's very worried about you, and after stepping just a couple of feet into your house I can see why she's worried. This place smells and looks like a pig pen, and you look terrible. Please, put on some shoes and come out to my car. We're going for a ride." He could have refused but the look in Nancy's eyes told him he better not mess around.

She seemed to know where she was going because she turned left onto Eastern Avenue without any hesitation. Within seconds Drew also knew where she was taking him. She was driving around the back shore of Gloucester to Seaside Cemetery where Shelly was buried. He started tearfully pleading with Nancy to turn around and take him home. She wouldn't respond to him and kept driving until she pulled up to the cemetery. Turning in her seat she said, "Drew, you're going to get out of this car and visit your wife and son's graves. I know you're in pain. You lost your wife and son, but Bob and I lost a daughter and grandson. Yes, you lost your wife and son, but this pity party of yours has to stop, and you need to get on with your life."

She was saying the same things he heard his mother say on countless occasions. Maybe it was out of respect for Shelly's mother that he opened the door and walked to the grave site or maybe he was just ready. Seaside was a small cemetery with a view of the ocean. Gloucester's rugged and rock bound shoreline made one respect how tough the fishermen must've been who settled this seaport back in the 1600's. He didn't feel any of that toughness now even though his ancestors settled this rocky island and his father fished the sea before the sea claimed his life.

Nancy led him to the graves where Drew looked at the two head stones and fell on his knees. While still on his knees he started tracing the letters carved into the stone. His fingers gently felt each letter that spelled Michele Williams Ashley, Shelly loving wife of Andrew and mother to Bobby. Then he crawled to the smaller stone and did the same thing to Robert Andrew Ashley, loving son of Shelly and Andrew Ashley. He couldn't touch the part of the stone that spelled out their birth and death dates, and when finished he laid prostrate on the ground sobbing and saying, "I'm sorry, I'm sorry, it should've been me, it should've been me."

The next thing he knew Nancy was on the ground lying next to him with her arms around his shoulders. At first she didn't say anything but after a while she asked him what he meant. Over the next half an hour Drew shared feelings he had kept inside and managed to tell her everything that happened leading up to the accident that night. He told her how Shelly was only in the car because he was too consumed with some financial reports. Nancy learned that Shelly was angry when she left and his last memory was hearing the car speed out the driveway. Again he said," I should've taken the car and died instead of her."

Nancy said, "I know how much Shelly loved you, and I know how much you loved her. What happened was an accident, not your fault. If you'd been in the car the tanker may or may not have been on the road but that doesn't mean you caused it. I know you aren't a very religious man but do you really think that if there is a God he would selectively choose to destroy families? It was an accident. We're going to miss Shelly and Bobby for the rest of our lives but we all have to go on. You would be doing a disservice to Shelly if you destroy your life because of her death."

To Find What Was Lost

They stayed at the cemetery until it became dark. When Nancy drove into Drew's driveway he reached across the seat and hugged her. All he could say was thank you for coming and how important it was for him to see her. He asked her if she had a place to stay and she told him that she was headed back to Boston and flying from Logan to Texas in the morning.

As she backed out of the drive he thought about how generous she was to come to see him because she heard he was hurting yet at the same time he knew how much she was hurting. He knew in all likelihood he probably would never see Nancy or Bob again. Shelly was the only reason for them to form a relationship. That part of his life was over, but he'd be forever grateful that she'd reached out to him now.

He sat on his front steps and thought if another person tried to tell him about the stages of grief he just might cold cock them. He speculated that people who talked about the stages of grief more than likely hadn't ever had to go through them. It isn't the same as earning boy scout merit badges where you can say that you passed on a certain requirement and can move on to the next stage. He had been stuck in anger and it was eating him alive. He realized as Nancy drove away that he couldn't stay in Gloucester and survive. He had to move away to create some positive change in his life.

Drew was an only child and his decision to leave Gloucester would be hard on his mother. Their family had always been small and his only other relatives were his mother's sister and her two kids. When he was a preschooler his father died at sea while fishing for tuna. He got snagged on a hook and pulled overboard. By the time the crew could react, it was too late and he had drowned. So even when he told his mother that he was planning on taking a trip and didn't know where he would end up, she didn't say anything. She agreed and said that she thought he had to go because he had too much life to live and staying in Gloucester at this time would only hold him back. Drew knew it had to hurt her but it also gave him a glimpse into what really is meant by a mother's love.

With new found energy it only took a week to empty out his house of personal belongings. He then talked to a realtor and told him to sell it furnished. If the buyer didn't want the furniture they could dispose of the items. He arranged for his mother to represent him at the closing if and when that should occur. His Mini Cooper was too small to travel long distances in and Shelly's van was burned up in the accident, so Drew purchased a Jeep Wrangler 4 door which had adequate room and was tough enough to go off road if that was what he decided to do.

After kissing his mother goodbye and promising to keep in touch, he was on the road and heading south. The first night he ended up outside Philly and stayed in a motel. On the road early the next day, he still didn't know where he was going so he kept driving until he ended up in Charleston, South Carolina. The town was hopping with tourists, and his first thought was that it could be a place where he could get lost. Drew pulled into a Hilton Hotel in the historic district and stopped for the night.

After carrying his suitcase to the room, he wandered about the historic district. The temperature was a little warm and there was plenty of humidity. The streets were covered with strollers out for a walk and he could tell it was an active city. Eventually, he got hungry and ended up back at the hotel bar. Being alone, Drew felt most comfortable sitting at the bar and ordering dinner, but he wasn't alone for long.

An attractive woman in a business suit sat down beside him and immediately started a conversation. "Whew, it sure was a muggy one out there today wasn't it?"

"Yes, it was."

"Are you visiting Charleston or here for work? I, myself, would love to be visiting, but indeed I am here for work."

"Oh."

"Well, you sure are a silent one. I guess you're going to leave all the talking up to me." Just then the bartender came up to the counter. "Bartender, I'll take the grilled chicken dinner with a baked potato and string beans. Also, give me a tall Scotch and water please." Once the bartender left the area she continued as she reached out her hand, "My name's Amy, and I'm here pushing drugs."

When Drew looked confused she said, "For some reason that's never as funny as it sounds in my head before I say it. I'm a pharmaceutical rep and this is part of my district. Now, why did you say you were here?"

Amy continued talking for the next hour and seemed to be satisfied with Drew's monosyllabic answers. It seemed like she was getting ready to leave as she turned to him and put a key card in his hand. "Room 317, and don't be late."

Drew had no intention of going to her room but as he was leaving the bar he noticed her purse on the floor. Picking it up he headed to room 317. He still wasn't going to use the key card and instead knocked on the door. Someone mumbled something and then he saw the door open. Amy was standing in front of him with a towel wrapped around her. As he handed her the purse she grabbed his arm and pulled him into the room. She dropped the purse on the floor and said, "When I leave my purse I feel like the big ol' witch making a house out of bread and sugar to catch Hansel and Gretel."

At that moment Amy dropped the towel and pulled him by the shirt to the bed. Drew didn't think he would be a willing participant but even as depressed as he was a beautiful naked woman turned him on. His clothes were soon in a pile by the bed and Amy left no doubt that she was in charge. Before she pulled him into bed she whispered, "I don't expect or want to see you here in the morning." She seemed to be very comfortable telling how and where to touch her and even corrected him if she didn't like his technique. He knew that he was in for an extraordinary night, and that it was.

Drew was thinking Shelly and he had a real good sex life. Unless she was faking it she always said that he totally satisfied her. They weren't overly adventurous but did enjoy each other's body. Amy on the other hand was like no other woman he'd been with and he'd had a few lovers before Shelly. She'd tell him if he was too slow, too fast, too soft or too hard. He had to admit the sex was great but that's all it was, just sex. There was no feeling behind it and by early morning he felt emptier than before he had met her.

Leaving her room in the early morning hours wasn't a struggle for him. In fact, by the time he got back to his own room he wanted to leave Charleston so badly that he immediately checked out of the hotel and started driving. By nine in the morning he was nearing Tennessee and feeling so exhausted he pulled into a rest stop and quickly fell asleep. A sharp rap on his window woke him from a deep sleep and he saw a State Trooper standing next to the door. After clearing his head he was able to give him his license and registration. The trooper said the rest stop attendant called, concerned that something was wrong because he had been there for over 6 hours during the daylight.

Drew was on auto pilot the rest of the day. He knew he must've stopped for gas, food, to use the rest room and to sleep but he really couldn't tell where or when. He drove through the night and the Welcome to Michigan sign was a pretty obvious clue that he must've been heading northwest. He thought it'd sound foolish to ask someone where he was so he did the next best thing and pulled into the next rest area. In the entrance, outside the rest rooms was a big map of Michigan with a star stating "You are here". He was in South Haven and according to the map, it was on the shore of Lake Michigan. But in reality he could have been on any interstate in the lower 48 because in many ways he didn't care what it looked like.

Chapter 2

As Drew stared at the map he realized that he was only a few hours from Manitou where Shelly had grown up. She never brought him to her home town because her parents moved when she was out of school, and their family home was no longer there to visit. They were supposed to go back for her 10th high school reunion but she had just given birth to Bobby and the timing wasn't right. Drew didn't believe in fate, but he also couldn't explain how he got from South Carolina to Michigan. Some unknown force had directed him that way but now he was in control again and he wanted to see the place where his beautiful wife lived as a child.

He continued driving north on a road that sometimes followed the shoreline, providing beautiful views and other times was a four lane interstate with large rolling farm fields on each side. When he arrived in Manitou he turned onto River Street which was the main street in their downtown shopping district. His imagination was captured by the two and three-story Victorian store fronts banking the sides of the curved downtown street like mountains following a river channel. The angle of the street allowed an exceptional view of the facades of buildings and although he'd never been here before there was something very familiar and comforting about the place.

In the middle of downtown there was an inn located in a converted Victorian office building that had a turret on one corner which stretched from the sidewalk to the top of the third story and below the turret there were stairs to a pub on the lower level. The pub caught his attention and his stomach told him it was time to stop for dinner. It was an enchanting place, and he felt as if he stepped back in time 50 years.

To Find What Was Lost

When he opened the door all the chatter stopped for a minute as the locals turned to see who was entering their domain. When it was clear to them that he was a stranger they resumed their conversations and only occasionally looked to see what he was doing.

Drew sat at the bar and ordered a turkey sandwich along with a craft beer from one of many Michigan breweries. These days every state seems to have a number of micro-breweries the majority of which no one has ever heard of outside their own state. The bartender was perfect. She let him know she was open for conversation but wasn't pushy. Before long Drew learned that if he was interested in getting a room in the Inn upstairs he could register with her. The longer he sat there the better the idea sounded, as he suddenly felt totally exhausted and all he could think of was a bed. With her assistance, he registered for a room and was directed where to park the Jeep so it wouldn't get a ticket.

There were only eight rooms in the newly restored inn. His room was on the second floor and was large with a sitting area in the turret that he had seen from outside. He didn't even bother turning on the large flat screen TV because the king size bed was calling him. Drew stripped off all his clothes and left them on the floor. The sheets must have been professionally laundered 1,000 count linens because it was pure luxury climbing between them. Sleep came fast and it must have been deep because he didn't remember a thing till there was noise from a truck on the street outside the window. He was going to give them hell until he looked at the clock and realized he had slept for 14 hours.

After using the toilet, he did some gentle stretching. His muscles were all complaining about their lack of activity. He finished off a complimentary bottle of water left in the room, threw on his jogging clothes and shoes and headed out the door. The clerk at the front desk suggested a jogging route that would take him along the river to the south beach and then back crossing the river over the draw bridge and going to the north beach. By the time Drew got back to the Inn the clerk said he'd have run a little over four miles. It sounded perfect.

Almost directly across from the inn were stairs leading down to a river walk. While looking at a map posted by the river walk entrance, Drew saw that he was entering at the mid-way point. The total length of the river walk was 1 ¼ miles and ran along the downtown shopping district, eventually ending at Lake Michigan. The wooden decking was actually a pretty good surface for running and there were some unique ramps and curves as it changed elevations at points. There were plenty of things to look at with boat docks and condos occupying the space along the banks on each side. As Drew got closer to the mouth of the river he was blown away by a sight of a huge freighter that almost filled the entire river from one bank to the other.

A small group of people were leaning on the deck rails while watching the ship move slowly toward its destination in the inland lake with all the factories. After a brief moment Drew became aware that he was standing next to another jogger. Without looking at her Drew said, "This is amazing." She answered, "You must be a lower laker virgin?" He turned and looked at her and all he could manage to utter was "What?" Drew found himself staring at the most beautiful blue eyes he'd ever seen, framed by black curly hair pasted to the side of her head by perspiration.

She resumed looking at the ship and told him that on the Great Lakes the freighters are called lower lakers. "They come in different sizes but most of them coming in to Manitou are about 700 feet long. This one looks like it is delivering coal to the paper mill or power plant located on Manitou Lake. Sometimes they come in to pick up salt from Morton's or chemicals from Martin Marietta. Watching the ships navigate this narrow channel is one of those things you never tire of. It's like the way you can't help but look at a rainbow forming after a rain storm. Well, nice talking with you, but I need to keep running."

Drew started jogging behind her while also admiring her body and running form. She had an athlete's physique with a slender but muscular body and all her movements were smooth and easy. She must have been a pretty good runner because before Shelly's death he usually ran 5 days a week but today he was clearly out of shape and having trouble keeping up with her. The river walk ended at the lake where she did a 180 and headed back the way she came. She gave a nod of her head as she passed and for the first time since Shelly died Drew wanted to know more about a woman.

He continued his run, and though he had to stop often, he enjoyed every step. As he passed by the south beach which was still without people, he was amazed that the parking was free and the lot nearly empty. He chuckled to himself because back in Gloucester you needed a resident sticker to park at Good Harbor or Wingaersheek Beaches or else you paid a hefty daily parking fee. The second half of the run brought him past the north beach and here a number of early bathers were already staking out a spot for their day on the beach. He felt the best he had in months, however, throughout the remainder of the run Drew was aware that he was looking in all directions to see if the woman jogger was still around.

After taking a long shower, he put on comfortable clothes and started walking around the town. Immediately he noticed the people were very friendly and more than once he was asked if he needed directions or if he was visiting town. By reading literature at the Inn and looking at the display in the museum window he learned that the town was old for Michigan and had an important history in the lumber and salt industries. There were a few lumber baron mansions left from the lumbering days but the coffee table book at the Inn reported that most of the huge mansions were torn down during the great depression. There used to be some commercial fishing, but the majority of commercial fishing industry was now through the local Indian tribe, and the more traditional commercial fishing had been replaced by the charter boat industry.

Walking back to the Inn he stopped and looked at a "for sale" sign hung on a beautiful Victorian block of three retail stores. The brochure hanging next to the sign indicated that the building had three retail stores and 6 apartments on the second floor. All three retail spaces were occupied which was a positive sign. There was a shop featuring a variety of hats for men and women along with other accoutrements. The next shop was a candle shop that featured handmade candles, and the last store was a specialty sporting goods store called "Silent Sports." He casually walked in all three stores and asked the clerks how their summer was going. What he found out was that small-town retail requires dedication and flexibility. More often than not the owners were also the clerks who felt they were responsible for promoting the town.

Drew was most intrigued by the sporting goods store because its items were something he was interested in and they were high end. The quality of the running, tennis, and walking shoes was the very best. In the rather small space they displayed many beautiful items that support sports such as running, kayaking, bicycling, tennis, canoeing and more. A trim blond haired woman came over and asked Drew if he needed help. He started out by asking about the running shoes, but in reality he was more interested in the building that was for sale. He knew that he'd have to dance around a bit before broaching that subject.

Trying to get more information he said, "My name's Drew Ashley and I'm visiting from out of town. You have a beautiful shop here. Are you the owner? I'm kind of surprised to see such high end merchandise in a little town like Manitou. I wouldn't have thought there was enough population to drive such an upscale business." He obviously said the wrong thing, or maybe she felt he was insulting her because she was almost snippy when she replied, "Thank you for the compliment if that's what you meant. In regards to our business we do just fine and our little town is very supportive. Now is there something I can direct you to?"

Drew decided to avoid irritating her any further and said he would go look at the running accessories. He found a whole aisle across from the shoes filled with the latest and greatest running gadgets. Drew checked out the compression clothing, headphones, and hats and then something caught his eye. It was a fitness watch that measures steps taken, distance traveled, floors climbed, speed, heart rate, calories burned, and pace, to name a few, all for $250.00. He had been interested in some of the new monitoring devices before Shelly was killed but never wanted to spend the money for one. In the year since her death the advancement in technology and reduction in price made him ready to buy, particularly after his poor running performance today.

When he asked the less than friendly clerk if he could see the most expensive fitness watch out of the case, her attitude did a complete reversal. She began telling him about all features of the watch and how many runners improved their times just by using a few of the features. She shared that she was a runner but nowhere near the caliber of her partner. Both of them use the fitness watch and she pulled up her sleeve to show him a lady's version of the watch he was interested in buying.

Drew told her that he had wanted one for some time and now seemed like as good a time as any. To let her know he was a serious runner he told her about qualifying for the Boston Marathon 3 times and running in it twice. She really started paying attention when he talked about Boston particularly when he shared that the last time he ran it was in 2013. Whenever anyone knows that a person ran in the 2013 marathon the next question is "How close were you to the bombs?" She then reached out her hand and said, "My name is Kathy Mueller.
What did you say your name was again?"

To Find What Was Lost

"Andrew, Andrew Ashley, but everyone calls me Drew," he responded. "I'd finished the race before the bombs went off, but I was walking back to watch my wife finish. Fortunately, she kicked off a shoe and lost some time. Otherwise she'd have been in the danger zone." After playing with the watch and allowing Kathy to brief him on the functions he pulled out his credit card and told her to write it up.

As he was walking out the door the woman runner from this morning's run came charging through the door. If she saw or recognized Drew, there was no indication as she ran up to Kathy. It was easy to tell she was very bothered about something. Drew stood there for a while watching the two of them. He could only hear bits and pieces, but it sounded as if someone had done something to her again. Kathy whispered something back to her and took each of her hands in hers. After a few minutes the woman left Kathy and went through a door at the back of the store.

Figuring the excitement was over he walked out to the sidewalk and saw a vintage Willy's Jeepster convertible painted cherry apple red. He had to stop and admire the vehicle. It was a perfect beach car and he often thought about buying one to drive around Gloucester in the summer. It was probably a 1950 and like new, as it had been completely restored. The canvas was perfect and he thought the body was in excellent shape until he walked out in the street to admire it from another angle,

Someone had keyed numerous scratches on the side of the car along the driver's door. At first, he thought it was a bunch of random scratches, but as he looked closer words started to form. One could easily read dyke, lesbos and muff diver. It didn't take much of a creative mind to assume that the car belonged to the woman who ran into the store. A passing driver honked for him to get out of the road so he headed back to the inn.

Drew spent a little time in his room learning how to use the fitness watch and before long his stomach announced that lunch was waiting for him somewhere. The hotel clerk mentioned a number of restaurants including a few with decks overlooking the river. He'd eaten in the Inn's pub and was looking for something lighter. The clerk pointed him in the direction of a coffee and sandwich shop located on the next block. Jimmy's Juice & Java was just the type of place he was looking for. He thought he only wanted a light lunch but ended up ordering a turkey and asparagus panini and a fruit smoothie. While eating he watched the other customers and could tell there were a lot of locals. He was sure that after sitting 5 minutes at a table with any of them he would know more about what was going on in town than he would from reading the newspaper.

Chapter 3

After lunch Drew continued exploring the town and ended up in front of an ornate Victorian house that was now the office for Manitou Realty. On a whim, he entered the building and told the receptionist of his interest in talking to an agent about a commercial building listed by their company. She helped him identify the building and told him it just so happened the agent was in her office today. Within minutes a woman entered the foyer and as she walked toward him all Drew could think of was Shelly. This woman looked like she could've been her sister. She had her hand out and introduced herself as Addie Manton. It took him a few seconds before he could respond by shaking her hand. She presented herself in a professional manner and had that air of confidence so typical of real estate agents.

Once in her office she pulled out the listing and handed it to him to read. She talked while Drew read the details about the property. The owner had died about a year ago, and the property was part of her trust. The trustee was now trying to sell it and the building's been on the market for over 5 months. The listing was several pages long because it described each of the three street level retail spaces and all six apartments on the second level. At the end of the packet there were a number of pictures of the stores and the apartments.

Drew was used to Massachusetts prices, when she told him the asking price was $425,000, he was quite surprised. All three retail spaces have current leases ranging from 2 to 5 years depending on the specific retail space. She admitted that only three apartments were rented at this time and thought that there was a need for some updating in the apartments. She told him that the retail space rent was currently $1,000 a month and didn't include utilities. The apartments currently rent from $500 to $700 a month.

Why he was drawn to this property was beyond his understanding, but he really wanted it. Clearly, he could pay cash, but he quickly figured that with interest rates as favorable as they currently were he could buy the property with someone else's money and have a positive cash flow even without renting all six apartments. After a few minutes of thoughtful concentration, he said, "So Ms. Manton, when would I be able to see the building?" She immediately replied, "Wonderful. I have to give the tenants 24 hours' notice, so is tomorrow afternoon at two a good time for you?"

The rest of the afternoon Drew spent learning more about the locale by driving around town. He was amazed at the beauty of Lake Michigan and the two great sandy beaches in Manitou. The sand was every bit as nice as Gloucester's beaches and the lack of people was a real plus. He drove north along the shore line for 20 or so miles and passed by more beaches as well as 2 small villages. They each had their own unique charm and seemed more touristy than Manitou. Driving back to Manitou he circled Lake Manitou which also has two small towns located on its shore. There were also three or four good size factories located on Lake Manitou. The lower laker that he saw that morning was moving slowly across Manitou Lake toward the river on its way back out to Lake Michigan. Although the population base is small, Manitou still felt like a working city and not so much of a tourist town.

To Find What Was Lost

That night Drew went to the pub in the inn, thinking of grabbing a quick meal and maybe a beer or two. The pub was about half full and again most of the customers seemed like locals. Sitting at the bar he overheard lots of conversation about town issues, like the cost of water, the poor roads and even some high ranking official that got fired, but overall everyone seemed in a good mood. When the door opened and he looked up to see Kathy and his running acquaintance from this morning enter and sit at a table. They both appeared very comfortable in the setting, and several people either talked with them or acknowledged them as they sat at their table.

Drew resumed sipping on his beer when he felt a tap on his shoulder.
Kathy was standing there and said, "Have you eaten yet?" When he answered "No," she said, "Why don't you join us at our table. After all we'd hate to see our newest customer and a visitor to boot sit alone in a strange town." There wasn't a question in his mind about joining them. He told the bartender to keep his tab going and said he'd be at a table, pointing to where Kathy was sitting. The first thing he did was introduce or reintroduce himself in the case of Kathy. He smiled and said, "Hi, I'm Drew and I'm a Lower Laker virgin."

Both women picked up on his jest and replied simultaneously, "Hi Drew."

He kidded and said, "Sounds like someone has attended an AA meeting in their past. Kathy, I remember your name from the store but I'm afraid that I never got your name this morning."

She looked at him with those gorgeous blue eyes and said, Hi Drew, I'm Tamara."

The rest of the evening flew by. The food was really good but the conversation even better. Kathy shared that Drew ran the Boston Marathon two times including 2013 with his wife. A lot of time was spent talking about races, in particular the Boston Marathon. Maybe it was because she'd dealt with him at the store but Kathy seemed to be leading the conversation. Finally, Tamara spoke, "I've always loved Boston from the time I was a child when my father took me there to watch him compete in the race. He came in 2nd one year but that was before I was born and before the Kenyan's were dominating the race. I have run in it 7 times and did pretty well for a white girl from the States."

"Pretty well, I'll say," said Kathy, "Tamara came in 7th for the women one year and was the top American woman finisher. She has been a world ranked distance runner and an All American when she was on Blue Water State's track team." Tamara almost seemed to be blushing at Kathy's comments and he noticed her gently lay her hand on Kathy's and say, "Enough about me. Tell us why you're here, Drew?"

Drew really wasn't ready to tell strangers his life story so he gave them the condensed version. "Well, I've lived all my life in Gloucester, a small seaport north of Boston, and the opportunity came up to sell my business so I took it. I had nothing keeping me there and lots of reasons to see other parts of the country."

"But why Manitou?" asked Kathy.

"Okay, here's the story. My wife died a little over a year ago and I was a mess. I couldn't stay around my home town with everyone feeling sorry for me. Selling my business happened just as I said. However, arriving in Manitou wasn't just serendipity. My wife grew up here as a child and she always wanted me to see it. Her family moved to Texas when she finished high school so when we visited her folks it was always in Texas. She said Gloucester reminded her of Manitou. Anyway, we were going to go to her ten-year reunion about four years ago but something prevented it."

Kathy spoke immediately, "I grew up here and my class reunion was four years ago. We'd have been the same year in school. I'm sure I knew her. In Manitou the locals always ask "what was her name from home?" I've never heard it any other place but lots of locals say it's from all the Polish immigrants.
So what was her family name?"

Drew swallowed nervously before speaking. Her name was Michele, but everyone called her Shelly. Shelly Williams."

Kathy turned white and was uncharacteristically speechless for a moment. Then she said, "Oh my God, Shelly's dead and she was your wife. I don't believe it." Tears started flowing from Kathy's eyes, "Sorry for the tears but it's a shock to hear she died. We were really close friends right up till the time she moved. We lived three houses apart on Fourth Street and just about lived at each other's house. Spring break of my freshman year in college I went to Dallas to visit her, and that summer she came back to Manitou to visit me. We promised we'd always be friends but we drifted away from each other.

I can't believe it. In fact, if you're going to be in town another day I'll get the old photo albums from my mother and show you pictures of her back then."

"I don't mean to pry but I'm in a state of shock. How did she die? Was it cancer?" asked Kathy.

Drew was stunned that Kathy was friends with Shelly and didn't know how to answer her question. He kept it simple, "She died in a car accident."

"I'm so sorry."

Sure he wanted to see Shelly's childhood town but he never expected to run into a personal friend. Within seconds a dark cloud passed over and he wanted out of the pub as fast as possible. He took one last sip of beer and said, "Well, thank you for the company but I'm going to call it a night. I'll let you know if I have time to look at the pictures, Kathy. Okay!" With that statement he was out the door.

Within minutes they each came to the conclusion that talking about Shelly was too hard for Drew to take. Kathy said that she probably overdid it when she started crying and then mentioned the childhood pictures and all that. She stared at Tamara and answered a question she thought Tamara was ready to ask," Shelly and I messed around once in junior high school and that was when I realized I was more interested in girls. For Shelly, it was just the opposite reaction and she realized she wasn't a lesbian. We stayed friends but were never lovers. Honey, I want to change the subject. We haven't had a chance to talk about what happened to your car again. I know how upsetting these incidents have been but you can't let them get the better of you. I love you and will do everything in my power to protect you, but you have to be strong too and fight these narrowminded bigots.

Tamara started to speak but stopped. There was a lump in her throat and tears were forming in her eyes. After she composed herself she began, "I understand that you think I don't have tough enough skin but for some reason you haven't been the target of their hate. All of the nasty phone calls were to me. The trash posted on line was directed at me and it's my car that has been keyed twice. It's wonderful to hear you say you love me but you aren't in school every day or on the track with 30 kids. I'm in the public eye and the easy target. On top of that you're from Manitou so you're one of their own. You told me that you came out in high school so the residents probably dealt with issues about you at that time. Now you are living with your lover and that is something totally different. It's one thing to identify a single person as lesbian, but it's more challenging for those same people to see a gay couple living together."

Kathy seemed to be listening intently before she responded. "We're here for the long run so people have to get used to us being a couple. It isn't like we flaunt our relationship. We're careful about public displays of affection. Last year when your girls' team won Regionals I wanted to pull you into my arms and give you the biggest kiss, but I restrained myself because I knew it'd upset some people. It pisses me off that we can't show love and affection like any straight couple. Enough of this silly talk. Do the police have any idea who is keying your car?"

"I reported it directly to Chief Parker," said Tamara. "Remember, two of his daughters have been on my track team and the youngest, a junior this year, will be on my cross-country team in the fall too. He didn't have an answer, although there have been rumblings throughout the county about that new church that opened in the old motorcycle sales building. It's some kind of right wing fundamental religious group that has taken a stance on lots of issues including gay rights, marriage equality, prayer in schools and of course protecting the second amendment. He hinted that if they are not directly involved they are encouraging anti-gay behavior. He told me that a 16-year-old boy from Wellston was attacked. Someone threw a hood over his head and he was dragged into the woods, stripped of his clothes and tar and feathered. It never made the paper because the boy's father was an attorney and his son went to a hospital in Grand Rapids to receive care and treatment."

Kathy looked shocked and replied, "I can't believe this is happening in this day and age, and in our town. We're going to check out this church. I wonder if PFLAG (Parents, Families and Friends of Lesbians and Gays) have heard of it. They still meet at the Episcopal Church on the first Sunday afternoon of each month. Maybe we should attend their next meeting.

Chapter 4

Drew's second night at the inn wasn't as comfortable as the first was for him. He tossed and turned most of the night. He assumed that it was about Shelly and Kathy being friends when they were kids, but he also couldn't keep his mind off of Tamara. Throughout the dinner, his eyes kept going to her even though Kathy was doing most of the talking. At the same time Tamara didn't seem to take any notice of him. When they did talk she seemed at ease, but there was no sexual tension like one often experiences when meeting an attractive acquaintance of the opposite sex. Duh, he thought, how stupid to think there would be sexual tension. She's in a same sex relationship and probably could care less about a male.

At dawn, Drew continued the same routine as the day before and left the inn for an early morning run. To his surprise Tamara was jogging in place at the same location on the river walk as she was the previous day. Today, she was alone as there were no lower lakers and thus no gawkers watching them. She smiled as he neared and said, "I thought you'd be running again today. Do you want to run together? It makes the run go by so much faster, and we can go as far as you want to run today?"

He laughed and said, "Good morning to you and yes I'd love to run together. In reality, I haven't been running as much for the last year so let's do an easy 5K. How's that sound?"

"Great, I know just the route that has a few challenges but also lots of beauty. Follow me." And off she went.

Who was he to question such a command as he watched the beautifully shaped legs pound the black top? Throughout the run he was behind her so he had the chance to focus on those long tan legs and the flapping of her jogging shorts. Her pace was faster than he was used to, but he didn't want her to know how much he was struggling to keep up with her. He kept pushing as she ran around the south beach, but instead of heading back to town as he did yesterday she turned south on Beach Street which was a long gradual hill. By the time they reached the top of the hill his lungs were burning, and oxygen seemed to be at a premium. Tamara looked back, and seeing that he was lagging, slowed her pace. She turned around and ran backwards until Drew caught up with her. He was too winded to even be embarrassed.

The next stretch was flat and ran alongside a golf course. She kept her pace slow so that he could recover. As they were running side by side he said, "You are one hell of a runner." She smiled and said, "Weren't you in the conversation last night when Kathy said I was an All American at Blue Water State? Oh, maybe she forgot to mention I was on the last Olympic team too."

"Okay, I've been had. You owe me a drink after humiliating me so," he replied. She turned at the next street and in a matter of minutes they were in front of Jimmy's Juice & Java. When he asked if she had money with her she laughed and said that they had her card. Once inside she spoke to the barista behind the counter. "Hey Rita, I'd like a 20 ounce, iced, skinny, fat free, very vanilla latte, and no whip and give my friend anything he wants. Just put it on my card." When Rita looked at Drew, he smiled and said, "Ditto."

To Find What Was Lost

They sat at a table outside to cool down while they waited for their drinks to be delivered. The silence was palpable, and after what seemed like minutes Tamara spoke. "I'm sorry if we hit a sore spot last night. It seemed that the talk about your wife really was hard on you. I know Kathy felt bad after you left."

Drew looked at her and said, "It was just so strange to be talking with someone miles away from my home who knew Shelly but at a different time and place. I'm interested in seeing the pictures. It's just that I couldn't talk about it anymore last night."

Tamara's quiet, unobtrusive manner made it easy for Drew to talk with her. He eventually started talking about Shelly, and before long he told Tamara everything about the incident leading up to the deaths of Shelly and Bobby. He shared how guilty he felt about their deaths, and even though intellectually he knew he didn't cause her death, emotionally he blamed himself. A tear ran down her cheek as he told her that he watched Shelly and Bobby get consumed by the burning fuel oil. She reached over and put her hand on his while verbally consoling him. He was afraid that if he moved she would take her hand away so he sat absorbed in the moment.

They finished their drinks but sat talking about things going on in Manitou and her job as a teacher and coach. Drew raised a question that caused her to freeze for a second. He asked her what she was so upset about yesterday in Silent Sports. At first, he didn't think she was going to answer, but then she started talking. "You know that Kathy and I are partners, right? I don't mean just business partners but life partners. Well, twice in the past month my car has been keyed, and the words are meant to specifically hurt and embarrass me because I'm in a same sex relationship. I guess we knew when we moved here that many people would have trouble accepting us as a couple, but the stuff going on is a lot more than not accepting us."

He asked, "Is it directed just toward you? You made it seem as if whoever is doing this is upset about your relationship with her, but Kathy hasn't been attacked. I also noticed that you said the problem exists because of a same sex relationship not because you're a lesbian. You didn't even describe yourself as lesbian, which to me seems to be the reason you've been targeted."

Tamara answered, "Wow, you don't hold back any punches do you. Okay, I'll try my best to answer you. First, Kathy grew up in this town and her family is well liked. Most people have known Kathy for many years but having a partner live with her was a new reality for them. They couldn't pretend that Kathy would someday marry the boy next store or just become an old spinster like so many women did in the past. I caused them to face reality, and they're taking out their anger on me. As far as calling myself a lesbian, I'll have to think about that. I've just thought of myself as a person who fell in love and it just so happened the object of my love is another woman."

Drew thought about what she said and tried his best to explain his thinking to her. "I'll be really honest with you Tamara. I could probably say that I've several friends who are gay, but in reality I don't. At least, I don't have any close friends that have admitted to being gay. So I'm probably really going to mess up this conversation with my questions. Before I met Kathy and you, I thought I'd established my opinion about the whole sexual identity thing. The two of you have caused me to stop and rethink it. I was comfortable thinking that gays were those people out there and so be it. Live and let live - that was my motto. As long as they aren't close to me what do I care? Now you've forced me to look at feelings that I hadn't considered. I don't know if I'm going to be around Manitou for long, but I'd like to think we could become friends. I'm asking for your understanding, particularly if I say or do something stupid with respect to your relationship with Kathy."

They left the coffee shop without any formal plans to see each other again. Their goodbye was sort of like saying I'll see you around. After showering and getting ready for the day Drew sat down with his laptop and did some thinking about the real estate property he was looking at in the afternoon. Depending on the percentage of occupancy it could be a good investment. The three store fronts looked solid, but the apartments were questionable. He was eager to see their condition and try to understand why they weren't full. He also took some time to call his mother and let her know where he was. She couldn't understand why he'd want to be out in Michigan while everything anyone could want was in Gloucester. She was sounding more and more like his grandmother who never left the island and questioned anyone's sanity who went over the drawbridge to the mainland.

Meanwhile, Tamara drove to the small ranch house she and Kathy rented together. As she was driving it occurred to her that she better not tell Kathy she was running with Drew? On second thought, why shouldn't she tell Kathy? The more she thought about it the more anxious she became. She wondered if Kathy would be jealous if she knew they were running together. Then it hit her like a lightning bolt. She was worried that Kathy would see her as having feelings for Drew. Fortunately, Kathy had left for work by the time she got home so she didn't have to keep anything from her.

After a quick lunch at a sub shop, Drew drove to the retail building where he was planning to meet Addie Manton. She was right on time and perky as ever. Thankfully, the longer they spent together the less she reminded him of Shelly. She gave Drew a thorough tour of all three retail spaces. They each had about 1400 square feet of retail with an office and storage in the back. All three shared a large damp and musty basement which was fine for storing items you never wanted to put out for sale again. Each unit also had separate utilities including electrical, gas, heating and air conditioning, and all were metered separately, which made things simpler.

Kathy was a little surprised when she saw Drew walk in with Addie. She immediately said, "Why Addie you didn't tell me the new prospective owner touring the building this afternoon was such a handsome feller, or is he your new beau?" Drew laughed and said, "Okay Kathy, you've had your fun. I just hadn't had time to mention to Addie that we're acquainted."

Kathy said, "Just teasing Drew. You know Addie and I go back a long time. In fact, we are fellow classmates of good ol' MHS. Now, is there anything in particular that you'd like to see in this shop or do you want to wander around?"

"Actually Kathy, I have some questions for you." Drew answered. He proceeded to ask her a number of questions about the business climate and concluded by asking her if there were any issues she had with the building that impeded her business. She responded so quickly that one would have thought she had a list ready for him. "Yes, the exterior is badly in need of a fresh coat of paint, the trim around the plate glass windows has dry rot, the heating and air conditioning are subpar so people bake in the summer and freeze in the winter and the trustees have not been responsive to our needs like when the sewers backed up or when the fuse box melted. How's that for a start?"

Drew said, "Thanks Kathy, I think I wrote it all down. We'll talk some more later. Good seeing you again. Say 'hi' to Tamara for me." Addie said her good byes and they were off to see the apartments.

It was easy to see why they weren't 100% occupied. The stairway leading to the second floor was dark, dirty and smelled like his grandmother's cold cellar. The walls hadn't been painted in years and the same could be said for the corridor leading to the apartments. The lights were single strand wire with an unprotected bulb hanging from them. Two of the apartments had two bedrooms and four were one bedroom. The two-bedroom apartments were spacious and occupied separate ends of the building. Everything about the apartments cried out for updating such as painting, flooring, kitchens and bathrooms. It looked like they hadn't been touched since 1950, but the bones felt good, and with a little work they'd be great spaces for young professionals.

The last apartment they went into was one of the two bedrooms. It was identical to the other two-bedroom apartment except it had a circular staircase in the corner of the living room heading up. Addie said, "I saved this for last because it's kind of special. At the top of the circular stairs she pushed open a cover and climbed out on to the roof. When Drew got there he was totally surprised to see a huge deck with railings, seating, garden boxes and a movable fire pit. It all looked grimy and he noticed nothing had been planted in the last few years but it had a great feel to it and the view was spectacular.

They went back to Addie's office and Drew asked if she had any comparables. It was a challenge finding anything to compare with this building since Manitou is a small city but they came up with one place in Ludington and another in Frankfort. Drew thought there was no way he was going to pay the asking price since there was so much work to be done in it. He'd also need to have an expert building inspector evaluate the building before making a final decision. Addie handed him a couple of names of building inspectors and then told him who she'd select if it were her decision. He figured the realtor got a kickback from the inspector so he took her advice with caution.

She then got up from her desk and said, "How about we take a walk? In the spirit of full disclosure I want you to meet and talk with other building owners in town." She led Drew downtown where they stopped and talked with several shop owners who also owned their building. He could tell the owners really liked her and were very open in sharing their feelings. At each place she asked the owners to tell him their opinion about owning a commercial building in Manitou. By the time they finished visiting seven shops, his head was spinning. They talked about taxes, lack of city support, the absentee landlords who allow their building to look like a slum. and the competitiveness between shops, but then they also shared about the great customers, the great festivals, the ways the shops do work together, and how much they love their city. For a moment Drew questioned whether he was insane to even consider coming to an unknown community and investing so much into it.

Since it was after 5 p.m. when they finished, Addie offered to buy his dinner and it was too good an offer to refuse. She had relaxed and no longer was the real estate agent trying to look so professional. For the first time since his initial reaction he saw her as a very attractive woman who was easy to be around, but she just wasn't his type. They went back to the pub which seemed to be the gathering spot for local professionals and shop owners. Over drinks and dinner she shared more about herself. Drew learned that she had a teen-age daughter and that she had moved back to Manitou a year ago after getting a divorce. She didn't say anything about her husband other than things just didn't work out. He appreciated her restraint because so often women have a great need to tell everyone how rotten their ex-husbands were to them.

Addie then became quiet and said, "In the spirit of full disclosure again, I have to tell you that I know about Shelly and in case you're wondering I didn't hear it from Kathy or Tamara. I don't even know if they are aware of your relationship to Shelly and Manitou. I did it the old-fashion way I googled you. It was pretty simple I just put in your name and Massachusetts. Up popped all sorts of information about you, including Shelly's obituary which informed me that she was the same Shelly that went to Manitou High School. So now I guess is the time I tell you how sorry I am for all that you have been through. I knew Shelly when she lived here but, she wasn't what you would call a close friend. So putting on my realtor's hat, I have to ask if you are really serious about the commercial property we looked at. The reason I ask this question is that you give the impression of someone trying to find something but you don't know what. Is your coming to Manitou just a reaction to Shelly's death and by being here are you trying to connect with her somehow? The commercial property we looked at is a big project, and it needs some serious attention. I'd hate to see you take it on for the wrong reasons, but if you're interested I can give you some names of contractors who can help with all the improvements and I'd support you all I can in the project."

Drew thought for a minute and then said, "Thanks for being so direct. I can't tell you if my motivation is pure because I got in my car and just ended up here as if I was on autopilot. I have to admit that the town and the commercial property really interest me. I also have to say that I don't know if this is a sad attempt to get Shelly back in my life. Shelly and Bobby were everything to me and life hasn't been worth living since they were killed. Since arriving in Manitou I've felt more alive than I have for the past year. Whether it's feeling connected to Shelly or not I don't know. I can tell you this. I don't want to lose the feeling because for the first time in a long time I feel like I want to live."

As Drew and Addie were finishing an after dinner drink, Kathy and Tamara entered the pub. Without asking, they joined

To Find What Was Lost

Drew and Addie at the table, almost as if it was assumed that they should. It was just small town behavior because Addie didn't seem at all disturbed when they sat down. Tamara grabbed Drew's arms and said, "Why didn't you tell me you were looking to buy our building? We're both so excited that you may become our landlord." When he looked at her he thought *I've got to do something to avoid looking at those blue eyes.* He found it difficult to talk while looking at her face so he just smiled. Tamara didn't look away this time but locked eyes with his.

Addie had to leave shortly after Kathy and Tamara joined them as she had to pick up her daughter. Drew stood up as she got ready to leave and told her he would talk to her later and was surprised when she leaned over and kissed his cheek. He was sure Tamara and Kathy watched the whole interaction but they didn't say a word after Addie left. Drew spent the next two hours listening to all their suggestions for the building. He kidded them about being full of ideas as to how to use his money but in all honesty most of their thoughts sounded good.

In the course of talking, Tamara said she liked running with Drew and missed having a running partner. She suggested if he was going to be around she'd really like to run with him on her three easy days. He couldn't refuse her blue eyes and a schedule was established. He asked them if there'd been any further problems similar to what happened to the car. They looked at each other and then Tamara said, "For the past few months we have been getting crank phone calls at all hours of the day and night. It's gotten so bad that we turn the phone off at night so we can get some sleep."

They denied being scared about the calls or car damage and wrote it off as an aberrant action by some narrow-minded slug. When Drew questioned whether there was an escalation of the calls they looked less comfortable. It seemed from their reaction that things had been getting worse. Kathy then shared that she'd heard from her parents and other friends that the new church in town was firing up their congregation about the immoral behavior of homosexuals.

Kathy said the Pastor is Ralph Hanson and he's been seen around town preaching on street corners while holding a Bible high above his head and a rifle in the other. She continued explaining that in his mind he believes he's taking a Biblical stand against the sinful homosexual agenda to change our country, especially their threat to children by enticing them into perverse and wicked ways. There're usually a few members of his congregation carrying signs saying things like" Civil rights are one thing, Sinful rights are another", "Stop homosexuals from seducing our children", "Marriage is between a man and woman" "Perverts will burn in hell", and so many more. I hate to say it but he's even caused some of the more mainstream churches to be quiet on the issue lest they be picketed too."

Drew knew it'd be phony to offer to help. What did he know about this issue and what help could he be as a stranger in a new town? He did say, "Well, you know where I am if you should need me." As he walked back to his room he did a lot of thinking about his own attitude toward gays and lesbians. In reality, it was an issue that Drew thought was someone else's problem. It was convenient for him to take a live and let live attitude because he never had to deal with a sibling, parent, cousin or even best friend who was gay. So the question he asked himself was why was he struggling now and why did his stomach flip every time Tamara looked at him with those fantastic blue eyes? He thought to himself that he must be coming out of his yearlong funk because in the past couple of days both Tamara and even Addie, at first, stirred feelings that had been dormant for a year.

It was while sitting in the pub with Tamara and Kathy that Drew made a big decision. He already felt as if he had a few friends in this town and being around his old friends kept bringing him down. A move to Manitou would be like having a do over. Everything would be new and the past was just that – past.

Chapter 5

Kathy and Tamara sat at the bar for quite a while after Drew left. Tamara spoke first and said, "I think Addie has a thing for Drew. Did you see the way she looked at him and that kiss on the cheek before she left? She looked like she wanted to drag him home with her."

Kathy didn't respond at first and then said, "All I noticed was how Drew couldn't keep his eyes off of you. There was one time when you both stared at each other and I wondered if you should get a room. I think he has the hots for you and if I didn't love and trust you so much I'd be jealous."

Tamara tried to act shocked and said, "What are you talking about? Are you worried that while we're running we'll stop and have wild sex? I think you're already jealous and for no reason at all. I've done nothing that'd encourage that man and you know I love you." To an unbiased observer one would think that she protested too much.

Before Kathy and Tamara drove home they stopped off at Kathy's grandfather, Frank Kraus' house, He was a kind old man in his mid-eighties and had been living alone since his wife died 6 years earlier. Kathy's parents still lived in town, but Kathy was very close to her grandpa and generally stopped in to check on him every week. Her grandpa had a chronic pulmonary disorder and was on several drugs to combat the disease that was slowly taking his life. He'd worked years in the coal fired power plant and he always speculated that the coal dust would eventually do him in.

To Find What Was Lost

Now he was close to 85, but not buried yet. However, his greatest fear was that he'd have to go to an assisted care facility. He didn't have much money and currently his children were helping to cover the costs of his medical expenses. Nevertheless, whenever he saw Kathy his eyes lit up. He loved the girl and because she loved Tamara he treated her like another granddaughter. However, when he was with his friends at the Senior Center he openly talked about how upset he was that Kathy liked girls better than boys. All of his friends sympathized with him but it didn't take away his sad feelings.

Later, as Kathy and Tamara headed home they talked about grandpa and whether he could remain in his home much longer. It was a discussion they had every week, and the bottom line was that he needed more care than they could give him on a once a week basis. Neither Kathy nor her parents had the money to provide in-home care for him so the discussion would continue until nature forced some other action.

They didn't discuss the situation with Drew any further but both of them were obviously thinking about it. As they climbed into bed Tamara pulled Kathy to her and started kissing her neck. Kathy's response was not what she expected when she said, "Not tonight Tam, I'm tired and have too much on my mind." They both laid silently in bed, and for the first time it felt as if there was a crack in their relationship.

Chapter 6

When Drew told Addie of his decision she was elated and pulled him into a hug. They kept that position till Drew felt uncomfortable and Addie handled it by joking that she gives all her clients a big hug when they make a decision to buy. Drew told her he would put 20% down contingent on the results of the building inspection. He also offered substantially less than what they were offering. It took about 10 days of negotiating till it was all said and done, but at the end Drew became the owner of an old commercial and apartment building in a small northern Michigan town. The building inspection identified a number of problems but nothing that wasn't repairable. Since he was expecting to do a substantial renovation and upgrade, all the identified issues from the Building Inspector would be covered.

During the waiting period Drew and Addie saw each other several times both professionally and personally. They had a few dinner dates and had become more involved than just business acquaintances. Their dates progressed from hugs to a good night kiss to one time when he almost asked Addie to spend the night. He didn't ask her because his thoughts weren't on her and it'd lead her on if she stayed. There'd been no promise of a romantic relationship but Drew knew he was playing with fire. Even though they both talked about how their relationship wasn't going to get serious Drew could tell that Addie wanted more than he was interested in giving her.

Before finalizing the deal, Drew talked with his financial advisor back in Massachusetts and told him what he was doing. The advisor actually had a few good suggestions that ultimately saved him money. He suggested Drew talk with the city planner to see what kind of State and Federal dollars were out there for a project like his. First, the city planner set him up for Brownfield funding which covered most of the cost of environmental abatement problems such as asbestos, mold and removing three unused five hundred gallon fuel oil tanks from the basement. The other windfall was some State money to defray renovation costs if four of the six apartments are leased to subsidized renters. The good thing is that after five years all the apartments can be rented again at market rates. Finally, the Financial Advisor recommended paying cash because it'd be easier to negotiate a lower price, and with the upgrades he was doing, the realty investment would grow at a faster rate than his current investments.

Addie was shocked when Drew told her he didn't need financing and this also made for a quick closing. His next task was getting a contractor that he trusted to do the work. He met with four contractors and walked through the project with them. Only two contractors followed through with what he considered a serious bid and he never heard from the other two but was later told by some other people that the project was too big for them. Apparently, it was common practice in Manitou for contractors to do verbal contracts with a shake of the hand, but Drew wasn't about to do that. As it ended up, Kathy referred Drew to her cousin Mike Edwards and he was the one who got the job. By the time the deal was closed on the purchase Mike had extensive plans drawn up. He had a couple of small jobs to complete before he could start. However, he also had a couple of younger workers who could start on less skilled jobs such as demolition.

One of the guys doing demolition was Jimmy Hanson. He told Drew he was nineteen and just learning the trade. His eagerness to work was apparent and Drew was informed that Jimmy was willing to help him after hours with his own project of restoring the two-bedroom apartment he chose for his own. He picked the apartment with the cool rooftop deck. The big time-consuming jobs in his apartment were renovating the kitchen and bathroom. Drew was really comfortable upgrading the plumbing himself. He had acquired some good plumbing skills to keep his car washes running since it was too expensive to call a plumber for every little problem. With Jimmy's help he made great progress in a couple of weeks. By the fourth week the kitchen and bathrooms had been remodeled, floors sanded and walls painted. It only took a power washer and some deck sealer to bring the rooftop deck back to life and now he was ready to call his apartment home.

Kathy and Tamara were always checking in to see how Drew was progressing. It was easy for Kathy to leave work and go up to the apartments. Tamara on the other hand was usually at school preparing for the upcoming school year or working out with the cross country team and track runners. She also had a full classroom load this year teaching earth sciences. So Tamara usually didn't show up at the apartments till early evening.

When Drew first showed them the rooftop deck they were impressed and immediately took ownership. With his approval they found some great beginning of the season buys at a local greenhouse, and by adding stringed hanging lights along with the plants the place looked festive. As they stepped back after turning on the stringed lights, Drew, Kathy and Tamara all said, "party time".

It became a regular happening for the workers, Kathy, Tamara and other shop owners to stop by the rooftop deck every day after work. It was becoming quite a gathering place, and Kathy was there most nights taking on the role of hostess. Drew made sure there was beer and soft drinks on hand but what he quickly learned about this town is that everybody pitches in. Night after night people arrived at the deck carrying beer, soft drinks, wine, chips, dip and more. Drew no longer had to buy anything because someone was always bringing it to the deck. Talk about a fast way to get to know people. In less than two months Drew joked that he was invited to more golf events, ball games and parties than in his previous 30 years.

Mike Edwards, the contractor, was totally invested and excited about the project and began to believe that he was playing a part in the rebirth of the shopping district. He was one of the few married men on his crew so he didn't join in with the deck parties too often. However, he was developing a strong work relationship with Drew and they worked well together. The usual strain that a contractor and his customer feel in the middle of a big job was not present at all. In fact, if Mike had an idea how to improve on the original plans Drew would listen and often accepted his ideas. The flexibility and sense of teamwork went both ways.

Drew also recognized that he was becoming pretty good friends with Mike. They communicated daily and Drew was really impressed with not only the quality of his work but his effort to keep costs under control. The renovation of the apartments was nearing completion and from the talk around town they were going to be some of the nicest in the area. One afternoon Drew noticed an unfamiliar woman wandering through the apartments with Mike. As he neared them Mike said, "Drew, I'd like you to meet my wife Edie. She hasn't seen the place and I invited her over. We have a baby sitter for the kids and I thought we'd join the crowd on the roof."

Edie gave him a huge hug and said, "Drew, you have done so much to improve this old building. I remember visiting a friend who lived here years ago and I thought even then the only thing this place needed was a good match. I also have to tell you how much Mike has enjoyed this project and especially working with you. All he's talked about the last several weeks is this project and how you both seem to share the same vision for the place. I know he's going to be sad to complete this job and that usually isn't the case."

To Find What Was Lost

Chapter 7

That evening Drew, Mike, Edie and Kathy were sitting around a table on the deck. Their discussion turned to the commercial retail spaces on the street level and the ways they could be improved. Drew talked about the list of recommendations that Kathy had given him when he bought the building. Before the evening was over Drew had contracted with Mike to repaint the outside, re-glaze the windows, put in new heating and air conditioning, update the rest rooms and resurface the parking for the tenants and shop owners in the back of the building. Drew seemed really happy that his relationship with Mike was going to continue and even joked that maybe they could partner up and find some places to flip.

As the summer started to draw to an end, the deck parties were getting smaller. Drew purchased a couple of outside heaters so those who were interested could still hang out. Many nights it turned out to be Tamara, Kathy, Addie, Jimmy Hanson the handy man, Mike the contractor and on occasion his wife Edie. Kathy and Tamara talked about being exhausted from the summer traffic and how they were looking for things to slow down after Labor Day. They suggested a blowout party for all the retailers on the deck Labor Day night. One look at Tamara's eyes and he couldn't refuse them. So Drew said, "As long as you two handle everything, it's okay with me."

One thing that was obvious was that Tamara and Kathy didn't talk or even look at Jimmy Hanson. Even when he tried to converse with them he was shut down. Finally, one day when Jimmy was helping Drew clean junk out of the basement, he asked him point blank. "What's up between you and Tamara and Kathy?" Jimmy seemed to have trouble finding words and then said, "I don't think they trust me. We've never had any trouble or for that matter even talked but they're leery and I can't blame them."

"What are you talking about Jimmy?" he asked.
Jimmy looked surprised and said, "Don't you know that my father's Ralph Hanson the Pastor? He's the one trying to get them to change their ways or in his words help them see the light and become regular women. What he really wants is for them to leave town."

"What do you think will happen?"

"My father and I don't see eye to eye on lots of things. He sent me to a military school when I was fourteen because he found I'd visited some porn sites on the computer. I stayed there for four years and only saw him four or five times a year. I survived the military school and, to be honest found it easier on me than living at home. The academy had strict rules but the rules made sense. I graduated last year and they didn't even show up for the ceremony. Oh well, as the saying goes God gave you your relatives but thank God you can choose your friends."

"Why'd you come back here?"

"That's a question I ask myself every day. Maybe I was hoping that he'd changed and wanted to get to know me. I knew I didn't want to go to college and I've always loved working with my hands so when the job opened at Mike Edward's Construction I took it. I rent a little house with a couple of other guys who work for Mike and I like what I'm doing. This is becoming my home and I'm not going to let my father ruin it for me."

"What about your mother? Didn't she try to protect you?"

"My mother took off when I was ten and I haven't heard from her since then. She took as much grief from my father as I did and just wasn't strong enough to fight him."

"Why does he have such a vendetta against Tamara?"

"He's always had a thing about same sex relationships only now it's gotten worse. You have to understand that he finds verses in the Bible to support anything he's thinking about. When he first moved to Manitou he had a run-in with Kathy's parents. He found out they were well liked and established members of the community so he backed off and wouldn't go after Kathy. With Tamara, he found his perfect target. She's an outsider, lesbian and a school teacher. All the stars were aligned for him to do his evil work. I've seen him do this before in other places. He uses people's fears to get them to think if they support his church he'll make their life better. You wouldn't believe how gullible some people are and how much money they throw at a person who panders to their fears."

"Do you have any idea who is damaging Tamara's car and writing the crazy notes to her?"

"I don't because I've nothing to do with the church or him, but I can tell you there're about six or eight crazies that'll do just about anything he says. He calls them his special council. I'm sorry to say that one of them is my older brother Joe. Joe has some intellectual limitations and never worked for anyone but my father. He pays Joe to do little things for him, and sometimes it's to use Joe's brawn when it benefits my father."

"Jimmy, if you could find out any information about these attacks I'd appreciate it."

That evening when Drew had the chance to talk with Kathy and Tamara alone he asked them what they thought about Jimmy Hanson. They were both quiet at first, then finally Kathy said that she didn't trust him. His father had done so much damage in this town in such a short while it was hard for her to think that Jimmy was any different.

Drew looked at her and said, "Kathy, you're expecting people to accept you as you are and not be influenced by any preconceived notion they may have about sexual identity. Don't you think Jimmy has the right to be judged on his own merit? As far as I can tell he has never said or done anything to hurt either of you, and I have to tell you I count on him a lot to help with this project. Until we're finished Jimmy will be working here, so you'll have to get used to him being around."

Kathy grimaced a bit and said, "You've got me Drew. And I hate to say it, but I've been prejudging Jimmy. I'll try to work on it but no promises." Kathy approached Drew and gave him a kiss on the cheek and reiterated that she'd try harder to judge Jimmy on his actions not his father's. Drew noticed that Tamara and Kathy were becoming more comfortable around him and not afraid to show their affection for each when they're with him. He thought he would get used to seeing them sit in the two-seat swing on the deck with one of their arms around the other one's shoulders but all he could think about was him sitting in Kathy's seat with his arm around Tamara. There'd also been times when they greeted each other with a kiss which is something they only did in front of people they trust, but for some reason this didn't bother him.

When they did kiss in front of him he wondered what it'd feel like to be on the receiving end of Tamara's kisses. Most times he'd shake it off and after a while he put them in the same category as his married friends. He wouldn't fantasize about kissing say Mike's wife Edie, who was a real looker, but for some reason he treated Tamara and Kathy differently.

The summer was flying by and Mike Edwards had finished bringing the four single bedroom apartments into the 21st century. He'd put in new kitchens, bathrooms and windows in all four apartments and overseen the installation of new heating and air-conditioning units. He'd also sanded the wood floors and laid tile in the baths and kitchens and was in the process of doing the same to the remaining two-bedroom apartment.

After thinking about the process to rent them out, Drew decided against taking it on personally and hired Addie's real estate company to handle the rentals. They took 15% of the rent but 100% of all the grief by making sure they were full and answering all the maintenance calls from the tenants. The four units that were rent subsidized were in high demand and the realtor did an excellent job of vetting the applicants. Drew still had the final word as to who would or would not rent but he was comfortable with their selection of tenants. There are hard workers in every community who earn very little money but still need a nice place to live without paying exorbitant rent. These are the tenants he wanted because they respect the property, treat their neighbors well and pay their rent on time.

The other two-bedroom apartment besides Drew's was one that he could rent at market price and there was a list of people interested in renting it. A big surprise came one night when Kathy and Tamara asked if they could talk with him alone. While others in the group were sitting on the deck watching the boat traffic on the river and enjoying the sunset to the west, the three of them went downstairs into the living room. The girls expressed their interest in leasing the remaining two-bedroom apartment. Presently, they were renting a small house out on County Line Road and they said with all the craziness going on they didn't want to be out in the county with no neighbors. Besides, it'd be really convenient for Kathy living above her shop.

The only reason Drew hesitated was because of his growing feelings for Tamara. He didn't know if he could handle having her live so close. Drew didn't think the girls had any clue about his personal dilemma and in their minds he was dating Addie. Lately, he'd only been out a few times with Addie and even dinner dates that occurred earlier in the summer were nonexistent. Still, he could see how they came to that conclusion, but his feelings were just not there for her. Drew never led Addie on, and when he told her he didn't want to date, she'd made it clear that she too was not looking to start a relationship after just going through a divorce.

At the same time Drew was wrestling with his dilemma, Tamara and Kathy had issues of their own. Kathy was pushing the move to the apartment for convenience and didn't think Tamara was supportive. However, both of them were impressed with the quality of the cabinets, appliances, and flooring. The house they rented was really beat-up, and the landlord had no intention of improving it. Tamara was reluctant but careful not to display too much resistance to the idea. Kathy had asked Tamara on several occasions if she had feelings for Drew, and each time Tamara denied any, but Kathy was certainly getting vibes that bothered her.

It only took a phone call from Drew to the rental company to reserve the two-bedroom apartment for Kathy and Tamara. The renovation of their apartment was nearing completion and would be ready within a few weeks. Once Mike finished there all he had left to do was paint the stairwell and corridor, put in new lighting and lastly put in new flooring in the corridor. Everybody who viewed the place was extremely impressed by the changes. The apartment project was the talk of the town even at Jimmy's Juice & Java. People Drew met for the first time were eager to talk with him about his vision for the downtown shopping district. Drew was beginning to feel like they were seeing him as the savior of downtown and that wasn't his goal at all.

The rooftop party that occurred Labor Day evening was huge. So many people showed up that it made Drew wonder if the roof could hold the weight. Everyone certainly had a good time, and toward the end of the party the Downtown Development Director corralled Drew and asked if he would consider having an open house for the community before the renters moved in. Actually, an open house was one of the requirements of the housing grant, so his request was not out of line at all. Within minutes the three shop owners on the street level decided to take advantage of the idea to hold an open house and make it a special sale day at their shops.

The day of the event Drew realized the renovation project was much more important to the city than he ever imagined. The list of dignitaries was lengthy and included the mayor, city council members, County Commissioner, the State Representative, Chamber Director and the DDA Director. The newspaper featured the renovated apartments in the morning edition, so a few hundred curious citizens along with business people were also there. The only place that was off limits was the rooftop deck. The city officials were very vocal about the project being the start of renewed housing above the retail space in downtown. The Chamber President spoke to those in attendance and said," One of the things I was excited to see is the potential for a live-work concept. You don't have to live there and work there but Mr. Ashley's building has the ability to create a live-work space that's small, medium or large."

The event was considered a great success and several people talked to Drew about other potential projects that he might be interested in. As much as Drew denied any interest in other projects, his self-esteem was heightened by all the comments influential town fathers were making to him. It must've had more importance than he let on because he did send a copy of the newspaper article to his mother and Shelly's parents. His thought in sending it to Shelly's parents was that they may be interested in what he was doing in their old hometown.

Chapter 8

A phone was ringing somewhere and it took Drew time to stir from his deep sleep and realize it was his phone. From the moment he said hello, he knew there was a problem. The voice on the other end was shaky and childlike and the whispered words were almost unrecognizable. "Help me Drew. I'm scared they're going to kill me." He finally recognized it as Tamara and it took him a few minutes to get her to calm down enough to tell him what was going on.

Tamara spoke in a hurried manner, "I heard some noise outside about 11:30, looked out the window and saw a lot of car lights facing the house. They must have driven up on the lawn. I heard guns being shot off and someone banging on my door and windows. I called 911 but the police aren't here yet. And now I see people carrying lit torches and wearing Halloween masks running around outside. Please come help me."

"Tamara," Drew said, "I'm on my way. Stay out of view of the windows. If you've something to protect yourself with don't be afraid to use it. I'll be there in a few minutes." He hung up before he remembered that he hadn't asked for her address. He knew they lived on County Line and figured there'd be a lot of commotion around her place. He pushed his Jeep to its limit hoping that he would pick up a police escort but to no avail. He dialed 911 and reported a problem on County Line but couldn't give the address. Outside the city limits houses were few and far between. There were no street lights and it was easy to get lost.

When he reached the intersection of Maple and County Line he had to make a decision to turn left or right. Drew thought he remembered the girls saying they weren't too far from the state highway, so he turned left. Sure enough he could see flames up ahead and several vehicles pulled off the road. He made a decision to drive like hell onto the lawn and see if he could startle them. As he pulled on the lawn the masked people started running to their vehicles. Wanting to create a problem for them he smashed his Jeep into the side of an old faded red pickup truck. The driver who was wearing a mask resembling Munch's *The Scream* turned and gave him the finger.

The Scream character managed to swerve his pickup away from the Jeep and drive over the lawn where he did a 180 before driving off. All the other vehicles were pulling out at the same time but he had no intention of chasing after them. They must've made a cross on the lawn by dropping oil because the smoky, flaming cross was blocking his view of the house. All Drew could think was that he needed to get to Tamara and that was his first priority.

When he got to the front of the house, he could see that they had stacked bales of hay against the door and lit them on fire. Running around back he saw the same thing at that door. The fire was already licking at the soffits and scorching the siding. The window closest to the back door looked the most accessible, so using his elbow he smashed it in. His adrenaline must have been running high because he didn't feel a thing as he continued to sweep at the window till all the glass was gone.

Drew yelled for Tamara as he was climbing through the window into the kitchen and started running from room to room. In the bathroom he found her curled up on the floor.

To Find What Was Lost

When he knelt beside her she threw her arms around his neck and started sobbing. Her whole body was shaking, and all she could say was thank you, thank you, thank you. They both heard the sirens and saw the flashing lights reflecting on the walls throughout the house. He led her to the broken window and was helping her out when a Deputy Sheriff ran up to assist. After asking if there was anyone else in the house the Deputy led them around to the front where two EMTs were standing near an ambulance.

As they were being cared for by the EMTs, two fire trucks arrived on the scene, and the firefighters had the flames under control in a matter of minutes. The EMT working on Tamara only found a scrape on her arm that must have happened when she climbed out the window. When they got to Drew they both indicated that his cuts would require a little more work. He hadn't realized how cut up his elbow and arms were from the glass. Fortunately, none of the cuts were very deep and they were able to use butterfly bandages with the recommendation that he see a doctor to be sure all the glass was out of the arm.

The Deputy returned to the ambulance and asked if Tamara and Drew would come to his car for a statement. Tamara was regaining her composure and able to tell him in clear, uncertain terms what happened. She said there were probably 8 to 10 men all wearing Halloween masks, running around outside her house. At first they were yelling obscenities and throwing rocks at the house. Then they poured something on the ground and started a fire. After a while they carried bales of hay to both doors, poured some liquid on them and started the hay on fire. She told the

Deputy that her partner was out of town at the Sneaker Summit, a national shoe convention, in Chicago.

By the time she finished telling him of all the incidents of harassment she's been dealing with, the Deputy looked exhausted. He was used to traffic violations. Hate crimes were clearly out of his league. Drew was able to give him very little information about the event but concurred that it looked like 8 to 10 ten men running around. They both had told him that Pastor Hanson at the Living Spirit Evangelical Church had been stirring up trouble for Tamara and that the Deputy should check on the whereabouts of the good Pastor. The Deputy took all their contact information and told them a detective from the Sheriff's Office would be following up on the case.

The firefighters had cleared the burning bales away from the door, and Drew and Tamara were able to get back into the house. Fortunately, the majority of damage was done to the exterior and the doors themselves. The interior was left untouched with the exception of some minor smoke damage. While Tamara packed an overnight bag, Drew was able to find two pieces of plywood in the garage that nearly covered the doors. As they stepped back from nailing the plywood on the front entrance, Drew tried to bring a little humor into the situation when he said to Tamara, "Well, it's not pretty and won't keep out thieves but it will keep out most wildlife. For what it's worth, back in Gloucester my grandfather used to say that any project using left over wood and looking a bit rough was done by a Nova Scotia carpenter."

As they were walking to Drew's Jeep, she noticed the bumper was bent and the fender pushed in a bit. He quickly explained how he'd run into the pickup truck, causing her to apologize to him for causing such a problem. Drew took her hand and told her she'd never be a problem for him, but some men in town better watch out because he's going to be a problem for them. Once she got in the Jeep Drew asked what motel she wanted to go to and she sat quietly without responding. Finally she said, "Would you mind if I stay at your place tonight? I just don't want to be alone and I don't want to worry Kathy. If I called her she'd drive back tonight and I know she was planning to make her whole winter order at the Sneaker Summit. I can fill her in when she gets home."

Drew was thinking that this situation was getting crazy. How could he have Tamara spend the night at his place with the feelings he had for her? At the same time, Tamara was terrified and wanted to feel safe. The only thing she could think of was being with someone she trusted to protect her.

When they reached the apartment, Drew told her she could have his bed and he would sleep on an air mattress in the second bedroom. He got out fresh linens and towels and watched her go into the bathroom to take a shower. While she was in the bathroom he changed the bed linens so she could get right into bed. It was going on four o'clock, and if they were going to get any sleep it had to be soon. Tamara came out of the bathroom wearing a crisp white tee and plaid pajama bottoms. Drew told her that she was welcome to any food she could find and she could set the alarm clock if she had to be up at a certain time. She again thanked him but said all she wanted to do was sleep. They said, "good night" and he went to the second bedroom to sleep.

Drew had shut off the light and settled down on the air mattress when he heard her call his name. He wasn't sure at first if he really heard it, but when she called again he answered her. She said, "This is going to sound weird, and I don't want you to read more into it than there is but can you come and hold me while I fall asleep. I can't stop trembling, and I just want to feel someone I trust close to me."

Chapter 9

Drew walked into the darkened bedroom and could just make out her body on the left side of the bed. Strange thoughts entered his mind like *that is the side Shelly always preferred and how can I stop her from trembling when just being near her right now is causing me to tremble.* He slid under the covers and laid his head on the pillow. Tamara squirmed backward till their bodies were touching. She then reached back and pulled his arm around her. No words were spoken but he knew she wanted to be firmly held. Immediately, she relaxed in his arms and as he was lying there all he could think was that she smelled like a delicious mixture of vanilla and orange blossoms.

She seemed to fall asleep quickly, but sleep came slowly for him. It took all his concentration not to become aroused with her in his arms. After a while he drifted off to sleep and was woken by the noise made from workmen out in the corridor. Tamara was still asleep and his arm that was still around her was numb. He gently backed away and hoped she didn't misinterpret his early morning hardness for something sexual. After leaving the bathroom he found himself brushing back his hair and worrying about how he looked.

When Tamara came into the kitchen, she still had on the tee shirt and PJ bottoms. Drew already had the coffee going and was watching Morning Joe on the television. She filled a mug that was on the counter and curled up on the sofa. There didn't appear to be any discomfort in her actions, and it looked as if they'd done this a hundred times.

She sipped the coffee and said, "I can't tell you how much I appreciate what you did last night. Just having you close by kept me from going ballistic. I know I was way out of line asking you to hold me, but I haven't been so frightened in years, maybe ever. Everything that has happened to me is creating fears, some from the past and some I haven't felt before. On account of everything going on in my life, do you think you can run with me every day? I think I need someone I trust close to me, and I know Kathy's knee won't allow her to run any distance."

"You can trust me Tamara," Drew replied. "I consider you more than a good friend and was glad that I was able to support you last night. Believe me holding you wasn't difficult to do and I'm sorry to hear that you've been in other situations that have shaken you. A couple of nights ago I bared my soul to you and yet I don't really know much about you. What's your story?"

Tamara took another sip and said, "My story isn't too complicated. I grew up in Flint where my father works for a bank and my mother is an administrator with the Art Institute. I have two younger brothers who are both in college right now. I had a great life in Flint. We lived in what's called the College and Cultural Area and it was a really tight neighborhood. My high school life was pretty uneventful, however, I excelled in cross-country and track and earned a scholarship to Blue Water State. Socially, I had a pretty normal life. I had a couple of boyfriends and am still close with some of the girls who were in my class."

"Okay," Drew said, "You've identified the elephant in the room so I have to ask about it. You say you had some boyfriends but now you're in a relationship with Kathy. I'm really clueless about this stuff so if I offend you it's through ignorance. But I have to ask, when did you know you liked girls?"

Tamara chuckled and said, "Do you mean did I have an epiphany and suddenly realize that I was a lesbian? It didn't happen like that at all. The simple story is that I fell in love and the object of my affection happens to be Kathy. Of course, it's more complicated than that but the bottom line is still love."

She was talking about some really personal stuff and he had to make a decision as to whether he should continue to ask questions. Drew realized there might never be the opportunity again to understand what makes Tamara tick. So he continued, "I'm guessing that the complication is your family? Have they accepted Kathy and you as a couple?"

Tamara spoke, "I grew up in a socially liberal family. My parents were and still are socially conscious Democrats. Do you know how many bankers are Democrats, let alone left-wing? They supported all the big social causes and marched in all the popular marches. However, they haven't accepted the fact that I can love a woman. It isn't like they have cut me off, but our relationship has definitely changed. We talk on the phone and I see them a couple of times a year, but everything is different now."

"I can't help but think there's something you're not telling me," Drew said. "I understand if you don't want to share but I can listen without making any judgment."

Tamara hesitated for a moment and then said, "The only other person I've shared this with is Kathy. I haven't even told my parents. I don't know why I'm telling you but some kind of inner force is pushing me to share it. I told you I ran track and cross-country for Blue Water State. During my junior year I fell in love with my assistant track coach. He was married and had three kids, but that didn't matter. I thought he was going to leave his wife for me. We'd have these clandestine meetings in hotels away from the campus. Maybe it was the forbidden fruit thing, but I found it very exciting. As I said, I honestly thought he'd leave his wife for me, and when that didn't happen I started to threaten him or at least let him know that I might tell people about our relationship. God, I was so young and naïve at that time."

"One day two of the male members of the track team cornered me in the locker room and dragged me into the equipment room. They took turns raping me but that isn't the worst part. The coach came to the equipment room door and witnessed the whole thing. I found out that he wanted to end the affair and was afraid I would tell his wife. So he either walked in on the rape or, I hate to say this, maybe arranged it himself. He did let me know that if I told anyone about the affair the two students who raped me were quite willing to say I seduced them and suggested a ménage a trois in the equipment room."

"I was embarrassed, ashamed and emotionally distraught and immediately quit the track and cross-country teams. I told my family I had a leg injury, but that excuse didn't work because they visited me at State by surprise and caught me coming in from a run. I never told them the reason for dropping track but giving up my final year of scholarship became a real sore point between my parents and me. One positive thing that happened was that based on my track record while on the team, and because of my results in the distance events, I was still invited to try out for the Olympic team."

"I met Kathy at Blue Water State and she helped me through the whole break up and rape. After graduation we went separate ways. Then we connected again when I was running the Bobby Crimm 10 Mile race in Flint. She was working for a running shoe company, so naturally I met her several times during the year at various events and we became friends. I wasn't expecting to fall in love but the relationship just took us that way. I know you're probably thinking it was because of my being raped but I don't think so. At least I don't think I have any residual anger toward men. I've found through experience that most men fantasize about lesbians but in the back of their minds think that all a lesbian needs is a good screwing. Oh, I'm sorry for letting my emotions take over. Please don't think I was directing any of those comments toward you."

Drew chuckled and looked at Tamara with a deeper level of appreciation for what she'd been through, but he didn't quite know what to say. "First, Tamara, I'm honored that you trust me enough to share your story. Second, your story is safe with me. I'll never share it with anyone and as far as last night goes I'm glad I was there for you. And, third, I promise you I'm not one of those men you were referring to. Now I think we have to decide what to do about your house and meeting with the detective."

Tamara said she was going to get ready and asked Drew to drive her to her house to get more clothes, particularly her running stuff. As soon as they left Drew called Jimmy on his cell phone and asked if he would get some plywood, a set of

hinges, a hasp and lock so that he could really secure
Tamara's house. Drew told him he'd meet him at Tamara's
house. It wasn't till later that Drew remembered he forgot to
tell him where Tamara lived. When he tried calling back he
wasn't getting an answer which wasn't unusual for northern
Michigan. There were lots of cell phone dead spaces.

The detective called before they left the apartment and
arranged to meet them at Drew's place at 2 p.m. Driving to
her house Tamara told Drew that she called Kathy to tell her
what happened and convinced her to stay at the Sneaker
Summit for the final day. She also called her landlord who
had already been informed of the fire and was having the
house inspected.

Tamara said, "You won't believe what that SOB said to me.
He said he learned the fire was caused by some people mad
at me and he didn't need tenants that brought trouble to the
house. Okay, he didn't quite say that. What he really said was
that he wasn't sure when he was going to repair it and said
that it wasn't going to be ready for occupancy for some time.
So he said I better find another place to live. I did tell him we
found a much better place to rent and he could shove his
dump of a house up his ass."

After packing her clothing, lap top, and some folders with
financial and personal information in her car, she was ready
to go. Jimmy drove in before they left and Drew got out of
the car to talk with him. He showed him the doors that
needed to be secured and told him to put the plywood on
hinges at the front doorway. He said to use the hasp and
secure it with the lock when he's done. Jimmy said he would
get right on it. As Drew was walking back to his Jeep he

passed Jimmy's truck and couldn't help but notice the older red pickup had a fresh dent in the passenger side door. Looking in the bed of the truck he also saw remnants of straw. All Drew could think was that Jimmy had lied to him and that he has the same beliefs as his father. Rather than challenge him here he decided to wait until he had him alone.

Drew followed Tamara back to his apartment so she could leave her car there. Then they picked up subs and drinks at a local shop and drove to the beach for lunch. While having lunch and enjoying the beautiful view of Lake Michigan Drew decided to try and get a better understanding of why she was being targeted by these homophobes.

Tamara could only focus on Pastor Ralph Hanson and said, "He moved into town the same year Kathy and I opened the store. His church is outside the city and they meet in a converted pole barn that once housed a motorcycle sales and repair business. It's in a really isolated area with lots of land around it. I hear they meet twice on Sundays and once on Wednesday evening, but I know nothing about their theology. We've driven by it and the parking area has quite a few vehicles. Most are pickup trucks with gun racks or old sedans with a door or trunk painted in a different color from the body."

Chapter 10

After lunch they drove back to his apartment in preparation for the meeting with the detective. When they got to the apartment Drew started carrying Tamara's things up to his place. She immediately told him to stop and tried to convince him to drop her off at a motel. Drew wouldn't take no for an answer and informed her that she and Kathy could stay at his place till their apartment was ready. Thinking she was worried about the sleeping arrangement, Drew told her that they could have his bedroom, and he would sleep in the second bedroom on the air mattress, since that bedroom was still unfurnished. Tamara didn't fight him, which was kind of a surprise, but maybe she was just letting him think he'd won.

As expected there was a knock on the door precisely when the detective was supposed to arrive. A big, ruddy-faced man who looked uncomfortable in a suit and tie was standing in the hallway. He introduced himself as Howie Stedman, Detective with the County Sheriff's Office. The detective wanted to talk to each of them separately, starting with Tamara. Drew told him that he'd be checking with the workers in the other apartments and to give him a holler when he wanted to see him. Stedman took his time interviewing Tamara and asked for her to start with the first episode of harassment and end with the fire setting incident.

Tamara repeated everything that she told the deputy the night before but this time the response was different. She got the feeling that Stedman was challenging her. He seemed to be looking for simple explanations, like do you think it was just a bunch of boys fooling around or do you have any boyfriends mad at you for living with a girl? He went on to say that it's pretty hard on a guy when a pretty girl drops him for someone else and it must be terrible when that someone else is a woman. Obviously, he was already aware of her partnership because he didn't ask if she was seeing anyone. When she tried to talk about the keying of her car and the harassing phone calls, he wrote it off as high school kids, probably boys who like you.

Drew could hear Tamara's voice when he entered the apartment, and she sounded mad. Tamara and Stedman both stopped talking and looked at Drew as he crossed the room to where Tamara was sitting. Tamara said, "I think I'm through with my interview. At least I get the impression from Detective Stedman that there isn't anything he can do." With that she got up and left the room.

The detective didn't seem flustered at all and chuckled saying, "She's a hot pistol isn't she".
Drew didn't know what to say at first and then asked the detective, "Why she was angry?"
Detective Stedman shared the same scenarios he'd shared with Tamara and told Drew that she just didn't like his conclusions. It was as if he was trying to find a harmless explanation for the incidents. At this point Drew lost his cool and said, "Detective, a woman's house was set on fire. She could've been seriously injured or killed. Her car's been keyed on at least two occasions and she's been getting threatening phone calls. This is a serious matter and should be investigated."

Stedman looked at Drew and said, "Look Mister fancy pants with that hoity-toity Boston accent, did you think you could come into town, throw some money into a building and we'd all jump when you speak? As far as I can tell, what happened last night was a prank that got out of control. I've spoken to the landlord and he isn't filing a complaint. So all I have is the little lady's complaint and that isn't much to go on."

Drew was steaming now and replied, "When I got to her house last night I drove my car into the side of an old pickup truck that was in the middle of the yard. I didn't get the number but I saw Jimmy Hanson, Pastor Ralph Hanson's son, driving a similar truck today with a dent in the side and straw in the bed. Why don't you do your job and start by investigating the Hanson's?"

The detective may have been overweight but he was quick. He took two steps across the room and grabbed Drew by the front of his shirt. "Mr. Ashley, I advise you to stop talking right now. If I wanted to I could drag your ass to the station and charge you with so many things that it'd keep you detained for days. But since you're new in town I'm going to give you one chance. I suggest you convince that sweet little thing that you're trying to help and that it must've been boys fooling around. Maybe her life would be better if she found a boy to fool around with. Do you get my point! We don't need her type in our town."

Chapter 11

Even after searching all the apartments, Drew couldn't locate Tamara until he went out on the street. Then he saw her standing across the street just staring at the river. He walked slowly over to her and gently called her name as he approached. Tamara turned when she heard her name and anyone could see her eyes were red and puffy from crying. Not sure of how to approach her and concerned that reaching out would be perceived as too assertive, he simply put a hand on her shoulder. That gesture was all it took for Tamara to turn and put her arms around Drew and start sobbing.

Tamara finally got her sobs under control and said, "Drew, I'm so sorry to do this to you again. You must think that I fall apart at the least thing, but that stupid detective all but accused me of over-reacting. The fact that my house was on fire didn't seem to bother him. I don't know if I can stay in this town any longer. Kathy keeps telling me it'll get better but I just see things getting worse. Why do people have such hatred for me? I haven't done anything to them. What are they afraid of? Do they think I'll molest all the girls of the town and turn them into lesbians? What am I supposed to do?"

Drew knew that she wasn't expecting him to answer questions that'd probably been rolling around in her head for weeks if not months. He held her in his arms a few more minutes and realized that he wasn't thinking about anything at all except comforting her. This was a change from the other times she was close to him when all that came into his mind were sexual thoughts. It was clear to him that things were changing in his relationship with her, and he wondered if she was feeling the change too.

Drew finally held her at arm's length and said," Tamara, your assessment of Stedman is right on. When I challenged his conclusions, the asshole grabbed me and threatened to lock me up under some cockamamie charges. Right now though, I've just the cure for the blues. You're going to get a chance to taste the Ashley burger with cheese, mushroom, olives, onions, and tomatoes topped with a secret picklelilly dressing. My grandfather taught me how to make the picklelilly and you're just fortunate that I visited the farmer's market this week and put together four jars just yesterday. So come on. We'll head to the deck just you, me, wine, hamburgers, chips and coconut lime cookies I bought at the bakery yesterday.

Once back in the apartment Tamara went to freshen up while Drew ran to the store for some additional ingredients needed for their rooftop dinner. When he returned he could hear her talking on the phone in the bedroom and assumed she was talking with Kathy. When she came out, he asked if everything was all right. Tamara told him she was filling Kathy in on everything that happened including the landlord basically kicking them out and the detective not doing anything. She did admit to feeling better now that Kathy knew all the details, particularly where she'd be spending the night.

It was a beautiful Michigan summer night. Everyone had told him the best time of year in Michigan was that time when summer is trying to hold on and fall is gently pushing her way in, and he could see why. The temperature was moderate, the humidity low and the white clouds were like puffs of cotton floating by in the early evening sky. He opened a bottle of Moscato and had already sliced some sharp cheddar cheese. He shared his limited wine knowledge telling her that Moscato is a white wine with rousing scents of rose, lychee fruit and peach. Usually, it is served as a dessert wine, but he found by accident that it goes great with a sharp cheese. They sat back in their Adirondack chairs and enjoyed the wine and cheese while the charcoal briquettes were heating up. Drew had installed a Bose outdoor wireless speaker system a few weeks ago, and the sounds of Diane Krall and other jazz standards provided perfect background music.

They did very little talking as they sat watching the sun move lower in the western sky. Although they couldn't see the big lake from the rooftop they could tell that it was going to be a beautiful sunset. Drew got up a couple of times to check on the coals, start the hamburgers and refill the wine glasses. When dinner was ready he called Tamara to the table and presented her with one of the juiciest hamburgers she had ever tasted. He also had changed the wine to Merlot because, as he told her, it'd go just right with the burgers.

It was as if neither of them wanted to speak because it'd break the mood. The sunset, the weather, great food and music had turned it into a special evening. As they were sitting at the table they heard the low mournful whistle of a lower laker letting the drawbridge tender know it was entering the channel. They had a perfect position to see the ship as it slowly made its way to Manitou Lake. The crew was busy watching each side and could be heard faintly talking with the captain through walkie talkies. The running lights of the ship sparkled against the blackening sky, and a number of people were gathering on the river walk to watch the event.

After dinner, as it was getting cooler, Drew lit one of the warming lanterns. He also had a lap blanket for Tamara once they returned to the Adirondack chairs. He opened a bottle of late harvest Riesling to go with coconut lime cookies. He'd never have thought of it, but the woman who owns the wine shop gave him the idea, and she was right on. The whole evening was magical, but Drew was also very aware that he was playing with fire.

When Tamara dozed off in the chair Drew knew it was time to call it a night. He gently shook her shoulder and together they carried all the dishes and leftovers to the kitchen. Tamara looked at him as she set three empty wine bottles on the kitchen counter and said, "Alright Drew, are you trying to get me drunk, because if you are you accomplished your goal. However, I think it was just what I needed, and I have to thank you for a wonderful evening." With that she put her arm around his neck and pulled his head toward her so she could kiss him. At first he thought it was going to be a good night kiss on the cheek, but her lips landed on his ever so lightly and stayed there a fraction too long for it to be an accident. She giggled and said, "Oops, I guess I do have to go to bed. Good night."

Drew cleaned up the kitchen and headed off to bed wondering what it all meant. Last night he spent the night in her bed comforting her. Now that she had kissed him would it be possible to control himself around her? He found out sooner than he ever imagined. Within minutes of lying down on the air mattress, Tamara entered his room and pulled the covers off him. When she climbed in next to him he realized that she didn't have on any clothes. She stuck her hands under his tee shirt lifting it up while rubbing his nipples. He felt her pert breasts against his back and her lips kissing his neck. This was just what he didn't want to have happen. As much as he lusted after Tamara, he didn't want her to regret anything she did because she had too much to drink.

Even Tamara wasn't sure why she went to Drew's bed. It was like a moth being drawn to a light. Everything about the evening was special and she felt a tingle in her stomach. It wasn't the way she felt about Kathy. With Kathy it was comfortable and their love-making was soft and gentle. She wanted Drew to take her hard and show her that she really made him crazy. She wanted to hear him calling her name as he came. Her fantasy all came to an end when Drew turned over and held her away from him.

In a soft voice he said, "Tamara, as much as I'd love to make love to you and believe me ever since I met you I've wanted you, I don't want you to do anything you'd regret later." Drew did one of the most difficult things he'd ever done, and that was to lead Tamara back to her own bed. He pulled the covers over her and then laid down on the bed outside the covers talking sweet nothings in her ear until she fell asleep.

Chapter 12

Drew didn't know what time he fell asleep, but the sun coming through the window told him it was morning. He focused on Tamara as she slept next to him. The cover had been pushed down to her waist and he could see her firm breasts with hard erect nipples. They were perfect and very, very erotic. His desire was to lean over and gently kiss and caress them, but his good sense told him to get out of bed and leave the room.

When Tamara came out of the bedroom an hour later she acted as if nothing had happened. She had on her jogging clothes and was surprised when she saw Drew in street clothes. He asked her if she was ready to run after the wine they consumed last night, and Tamara laughed and said that was why she really needed to break a big sweat right now. Drew changed quickly and they were in the middle of their run when Tamara said, "Thanks for what you did last night." Drew said, "What?"
Tamara replied, "You know what I mean." And that was that. No more talk about their near romantic tryst.

As she ran along their route, Tamara kept thinking about her attraction to Drew. She remembered the two nights they shared in bed. There was no sex involved but when she thought about it her memories were very erotic. She didn't know what she would feel if Drew had accepted her brazen invitation. Instead, he gently led her in all her nakedness back to her own bed. If she felt anything, it was guilt that she'd been so close to cheating on Kathy. She didn't feel guilty about desiring a man but did feel as if she violated her trusting relationship with Kathy. It was no different than what most married men would feel if they stole a kiss or more from a co-worker at their Christmas party.

Drew brought Tamara out of her daydream by asking her when Kathy was getting home. It took her a second to get her wits about her and she told him that Kathy should be home by 8:00 pm. She qualified the statement by adding, "that's if she gets away from Chicago by three". He then surprised her by asking if she'd have time to show him the high school after their run. Drew added that if he was going to be living here he wanted to become familiar with all the public spaces. Tamara hesitated for a moment and then said that she'd love to show him the complex.

Tamara gave him the complete tour, including the new swimming pool and exercise room. He was surprised that everyday citizens could use the track around the gym and also use the swimming pool. There were a number of things he liked about the community, and one of them was public access to the beaches, parks, river and now the schools. She waited till the end of the tour before she showed him her classroom and office. On the way there she stopped at the main office to pick up any mail or messages. The office secretary was the only staff person in the building and she seemed to be avoiding Tamara. Even when Tamara introduced Drew, the secretary didn't establish eye contact. Tamara didn't look at any of her mail until she reached her office at which time she scanned the material. One envelope caught her attention because it came from the superintendent's office.

Tamara gingerly opened the letter and stared at it for a long time. If a person could be a pot ready to boil over, that person would be Tamara. Drew could see her face changing shades and then she finally sputtered in an angry voice, "I can't believe it. Those S.O.B's aren't going to leave me alone. This is just too much." Drew reached his hand out and Tamara gave him the letter. It was brief enough but what it said would cause concerns for anybody.

Dear Ms. Elwell:

The Manitou School Board and the Superintendent request your appearance at a special hearing to answer questions that surfaced when morality charges were filed against you by a number of parents. There is significant concern about these charges that the board recommends you be represented by counsel. You are responsible for obtaining personal counsel if you so desire. The teacher's union has been notified of this meeting and will be represented at the hearing as well. The meeting will take place in the school library on September 8th at 7:00 pm. If you have any questions about this letter please contact my office.

Sincerely,
Robert Bowler, Superintendent

The anger soon turned to tears and Tamara started sobbing. In a gesture that was becoming all too familiar Drew wrapped his arms around her and held her against his chest. With her head on his chest he again smelled the wonderful aroma of orange blossoms and vanilla emanating from her hair. He hated to see her in pain but loved holding her. When the sobs subsided he walked her out to his car and they drove. It didn't matter where they were driving as long as the car was moving. All the while Tamara sat in the passenger seat with her head against the window.

Finally, she spoke, "I don't know how I can fight them. It has to be Rev. Hanson's church members because I'm not aware of any other people having problems with me. Drew, you have to believe me when I say that I've done nothing but try to be the best teacher and coach in Michigan. I'm not a pedophile or a pervert. I'm not attracted to high school girls and I can't believe that any girls on my team would accuse me of any wrongdoing. What evidence would they have that could cause this hearing?"

Drew didn't try to explain away the situation and he knew she wasn't looking for answers from him. He only said one thing to her and that was that he had her back. Drew wanted Tamara to know that no matter what, he believed her and would support her in any way possible.

After they had driven south past Ludington on Lakeshore Drive he saw a sign advertising fresh fish. It reminded him of home, where so many fish, clam and lobster places were just shacks where you ate at picnic tables with a supply of paper towels. At home, they called it eating in the rough. The sign said the place was owned by the same family for over 100 years and all they did was sell fresh fish or fry it to be eaten outside on picnic tables. Drew didn't bother to ask Tamara and pulled in front of the shack. He jumped out of the car and went inside. When he came out he had a large sack and two bottles of water. He jumped back in the car and drove about 50 yards to the entrance of a county park. The park road was about 1/4 mile long and ended on the shore of Lake

Michigan. There were numerous picnic tables on the property that overlooked the lake and a path leading down to the beach.

Drew got out of the car and went to a picnic table where he started unpacking the sack. By the time Tamara got to the table he had paper plates set out with plastic ware. Drew said, "Okay, the owner recommended this spot. We have whitefish, perch, catfish and I had to try their clams. I also have onion rings and French fries. There's lots of tartar sauce, catsup and salt. Don't be shy. Dig in."

Tamara looked at the selection and said, "Drew, everything here is fried." He smiled and said, "Isn't that why we run so we can eat bad food and drink good wine? Now I have to try one of the clams." He spit it out as soon as it entered his mouth. "These are like clam strips and bad ones at that. How can they possibly call them fried clams without the bellies?"

He finally got Tamara to laugh and before long they were both enjoying the fish. Drew even said that it was delicious, minus the clams of course. Tamara told him that she'd lived in Manitou for a few years and never been here before. The county park was evidently a popular place to eat the fish store's food because they noticed several tables were occupied by people eating fried fish.

Drew said, "Next time we come we'll have to bring wine, a table cloth and dessert. The lady inside told me that lots of people come prepared for a full picnic less the fish."

As they were enjoying watching the activities on the beach they both were thinking about his statement. What 'next time' was Drew talking about? Was he assuming that Kathy, Tamara and Drew would come the next time? They both were aware that his statement was challenging at best.

Drew started carrying the refuse to the trash barrels and Tamara went back to his Jeep. When Drew walked around to the passenger door, he first acted as if he was going to use his key to open it. Then he stopped, put his left arm around her waist and pulled her close to him. With his right hand he tilted her head up and made eye contact with her. When she didn't look away Drew took it as permission to bend down and kiss her lips. At first he thought she was going to back away but then she opened her mouth slightly and ran her tongue over his lips. He responded by opening his mouth and playing tag with her tongue. The kiss could have lasted for a minute or an hour. Neither of them had a clue. Time stood still for both of them until Tamara put her hands on his chest and pushed him back.

The ride back to Manitou was quiet until Tamara spoke, "Drew, you know I'm with Kathy. I love her and there can't be anything between you and me."

Drew waited a second and then said, "Tamara, whether you like it or not there's something between us. I feel it and I believe you feel it. I don't know how this gets resolved, but I've lost someone before and I don't want to lose you." When they stopped in front of the apartment building, Tamara put her arm around Drew's neck and gave him a kiss that certainly didn't feel as if she wanted to end their relationship.

Chapter 13

Over sixty men, women and children were packed in the converted motorcycle sales building to hear Pastor Hanson. The room was hot and stuffy but the people gathered in the old building didn't seem to mind it a bit as long as there were enough folding chairs to accommodate them. The Wednesday night service usually focused on the sins of the community and how it wasn't the mission of the church to save the sinners if they refused to be redeemed. Pastor Hanson regularly preached that gays and lesbians were already doomed to hell and righteous Christians had to rid the world of them.

An overweight pianist with sweat running down his brow led the congregation in several Christian songs, ending with "Onward Christian Soldiers". The pianist was accompanied by a couple of guitars and a drummer. The music wasn't the greatest, but the loud beating rhythm of the drummer created a responsive emotive reaction in the congregation. People were dancing in the aisles and waving their hands above their heads. You would've thought they were at a Rolling Stones concert the way they were reacting.

When the crowd was sufficiently stirred up, the pianist invited Pastor Hanson to the pulpit. The good pastor was on the short side probably no taller than 5'5" with thick wavy hair, broad shoulders and very narrow hips. Everyone knew he was very muscular because he always took his jacket off while preaching and chose to wear tight short sleeve shirts which emphasized his large biceps. Pastor Hanson started his message by saying, "Brothers and sisters, the world and the United States are being overwhelmed by a Sodom and Gomorrah spirit just as Jesus prophesied about the last days.

We're now seeing America, the largest, most powerful, most prestigious nation the planet has ever seen, founded upon the word of God, the supporter of Israel until you know who's administration, declare that we are the Sodom and Gomorrah, and we are going to export it to the world."

"Gay rights advocates are going after your children. How are they going to do it? They're using the public schools. You heard me. They're using common core to turn this nation into a gay nation. Your child's at risk of becoming gay unless you're willing to do something about it. Our own high school has already become a partner in this takeover, not only by participating in common core but by hiring gay teachers. Oh, it's a clever strategy because these teachers know how to appeal to the children. They win the children over and then turn them gay. Why, our high school has several gay teachers but the biggest advocate for the gay agenda is none other than that egotistical track and cross-country coach Tamara Elwell."

"Do we have to stand by and watch this? Of course not. Several actions have already been taken by concerned citizens. A group of these concerned people visited her home and tried to convince her to leave just last week. Now the sheriff is out asking questions about what happened, and you have to let him know that concerned Christians were only trying to convince the devil to leave our community. Another group of parents have petitioned the school board about Ms. Elwell's personal behavior and morals. I have it from a good source that she talks to our young impressionable girls about the joys of loving another woman. Who knows what else she's trying to do when your daughters are in the shower room."

"It's time for action if we're to save our children and this community. God's expecting nothing less of you. My Special Council has been doing God's work with this woman, and thus far she's rejected our plea for her to leave this community. I've asked God if she can be saved and God directed me to First Corinthians 6:9. God's word says do you not know that the unrighteous will not inherit the kingdom of God? Do not be deceived; neither the immoral, nor idolaters, nor adulterers, nor effeminates, nor sexual perverts, will inherit the kingdom of God."

"This is war and she's our enemy. During times of war people do things that are outside their comfort zone. Are you ready to go to war? If you don't act your children are at risk of becoming homosexual and they'll never be able to join you in God's kingdom. Is that what you want? The moral values we live by in this community are going to deteriorate, and life as we know it won't exist. God has spoken to me and I'm giving you his message. Go to the school board meeting and let them know there's no place in our school or town for a morally corrupt person. May God be with us as we go forth to battle. Now join our voices together and sing John Monsell's old hymn "Fight the Good Fight with All Thy Might".

The congregation joined with the thumping piano in singing a tune that was familiar to them. Most of the people didn't even have to look at their hymnals as they sang.

Fight the good fight with all thy might!
Christ is thy strength, and Christ thy right;

To Find What Was Lost

Lay
hold
on life,
and it
shall
be Thy
joy
and
crown
eterna
lly.

Following the song there was a reminder that God's mission
also needed money to be successful and parishioners were
urged to put their money in a large pot at the rear of the
sanctuary as they left the church. After the congregation left
the building Pastor Hanson picked up the pot and retreated
to his office where several of special council members were
waiting. Two of the men took the pot and started counting
the money while Pastor
Hanson asked whether anyone had seen Tamara Elwell lately.
Howard Stedman, the detective with the Sheriff's
department, cleared his throat before talking. "I interviewed
both Elwell and that new guy in town who bought the Wilson
block. His name is Andrew Ashley and he's the same man
who came driving onto her lawn to rescue her the other
night. I think they're getting pretty cozy because she's been
staying at his apartment. She doesn't care who she's
fornicating with that's for sure. Anyway, they don't know
anything, although they complained about you, Pastor
Hanson. Ashley also told me he saw a red pickup truck the
night of the fire that he swears was Jimmy's and he wants me
to question him."

Pastor Hanson responded, "Jimmy wasn't anywhere near their house that night so there's nothing to his claims."

Stedman replied pointing to another man, "Remember, Jimmy let Joe borrow the truck. Joe told him he had to pick up some straw for his horses and returned the truck before midnight. The question I have is whether Jimmy will let sleeping dogs lie or will he challenge what Joe did with the truck. Ashley dented in the side door and Jimmy already complained to Joe about it. Pastor, you may need to deal more directly with Jimmy. I see him as the weak link in the alibis. I can handle both Ashley and Elwell. I've already told them that I thought teenagers were pulling a prank and my investigation has found nothing more"

Joe Hanson spoke next and said, "I hear what you are saying Howie but let me add that a few of us have an idea about how to move this thing along, and the less information shared the better. All I will say is that this Ashley guy has to be taken out of the picture and we have ideas about it." The meeting broke up shortly after that and Joe walked out with two other men. They stood outside for fifteen minutes talking and all shook hands when they parted.

Chapter 14

Kathy seemed quiet ever since returning from Chicago. They talked about business, the fire and the school board hearing, but they didn't talk about their feelings for each other. It'd been four days and they hadn't made love, which was unusual for them. Tamara chalked it up to the pressure they were feeling about the fire and the school board hearing. Kathy explained it away by saying how guilty she felt that she wasn't there to help Tamara deal with the problems. Tamara didn't talk much about the role Drew played in supporting her because she knew it would not be received well. Since they were still living in Drew's apartment many phases of their home lives were out of kilter.

It was on the fourth night when their self-imposed celibacy was broken. After they were both in bed Kathy put her arms around Tamara and got in a spooning position. After making love they laid curled in each other's arms and finally they talked about real things. Tamara shared that she's afraid for her life. The night when the masked men were running around the house and trying to burn it down made her aware that it was not simple harassment. They meant to do her harm. Now they're going after her livelihood and all because they didn't like who she loved. Kathy talked about how powerless she felt being in Chicago and how she felt envious of Drew being able to come to her rescue. Tears formed in her eyes as she told Tamara how she had wanted to jump in the car and drive back to Michigan.

In the middle of the night a ding woke Tamara from her sleep. She looked over and saw that Kathy was sound asleep. She quietly got out of bed, and in the dim light saw that

Kathy had forgotten and left her cell phone on the dresser, but not in sleep mode. Tamara picked it up and went into the living room. What she saw on the phone surprised her. It was a text from someone named Alexa and simply said, "Haven't heard from u. Hope all is well, Miss u lots, LOL Alexa." Tamara's mind was going a mile a minute. "Who was Alexa?, Why does she miss Kathy? Why hasn't Kathy contacted her? Why LOL, was it laugh out loud or lots of love?'

Her thoughts were interrupted when she heard someone clear their throat and turning around, she saw Drew staring at her. Drew asked, "Everything all right?" Tamara nodded yes but Drew knew something wasn't right. He continued to stare at her, and it was then she realized he was shirtless and in boxer shorts and she was only wearing a really thin T-shirt and panties. Drew walked toward the kitchen and asked if she'd like a cup of hot chocolate?

Tamara watched him prepare their drinks and her eyes were glued to his back. The skin looked so smooth and the muscles so defined. All she wanted to do was reach out and touch him. Drew was struggling with similar thoughts. He was hoping that making a drink would take his mind off her, but it didn't. He turned just as she reached for him and they were in each other's arms. They stayed for a long while in a warm embrace, each struggling with their own issues.

Drew spoke first and said, "What am I to do? You must know I want to make love to you so much, but all I can think about is what it would do to you and Kathy. When Shelly died I didn't think I'd feel this way about another woman and then you came into my life. I never in my wildest dreams thought that if I felt something for a woman again I'd have to compete for her love with a woman. You have me spinning in circles and I don't see any way to stop." Drew broke away and returned to his room leaving his unfinished hot chocolate on the counter.

The next morning just like clockwork Drew and Tamara were awake and ready for their morning run. It had become routine and even their middle of the night get together didn't break the routine. They ran their regular route around the beach and up Beach Street by the golf course. It was a little foggy making the visibility poor, but overall both were running smoothly. Just when they were ready to turn back toward town three men wearing ski masks ran from behind the bushes that edged the street beside the golf course. One man grabbed Tamara and threw her to the ground. It was a struggle to contain her and finally he knocked her head on the pavement and knelt on her, which restricted her breath. Tamara's screams were stifled when he pulled by her sports bra up and forced it across her mouth.

The other two men jumped Drew and although he tried to fight them it was a losing battle. The larger of the two men swung a golf club and hit Drew full force in the shin. The crack could be clearly heard as Drew's leg gave out. He was clutching his right leg and fell on the ground. This allowed the man to take another swing and connect with Drew's head. He lost consciousness at that time, which was probably a good thing because he was hit several more times in the head and torso. They must have figured that Drew was dead because one of them said, "He's done for. Let's get out of here."

Tamara was in a state of shock, but finally pulled herself together and ran to Drew. He was bleeding profusely from the head and at first, she didn't think he was breathing until she heard shallow breaths. She gasped when she saw white bone protruding from his lower leg and that cleared her head like a whiff of ammonia. She looked for the men and didn't see them, but in the distance she heard a vehicle start up. Tamara saw Drew's eyes flicker open but he showed no sign of awareness. She told Drew not to move even though she knew he was really unconscious and then ran to the closest house. Banging on the door she woke a sleepy-eyed woman who reacted quickly when Tamara told her she and a friend were attacked and he was seriously injured. Tamara lucked out by picking this particular house because the owner was a nurse and showed great composure under the circumstances.

Chapter 15

After a quick call to 911, the good Samaritan grabbed some towels and a blanket and ran to Drew. She located the cuts first and told Tamara to press a towel against the head wound. She wrapped another towel around an open wound on his leg and finally as gently as she could she covered him with a blanket. She told Tamara that he was going into shock and it was best to keep him warm. She also said that without knowing the extent of the injuries she didn't want to move him, at least until his neck is stabilized.

Within five minutes the first responders from the fire station were on the scene, and a city police car arrived shortly after them. The EMTs were very proficient and in direct communication with the hospital. They prepared Drew to be transported to the emergency room and assisted the ambulance EMTs in loading both Drew and Tamara into the vehicle. The city police officer had taken pictures of the scene while Drew was on the ground, and he also got some basic information from Tamara and the citizen who assisted them. He told Tamara that he'd follow them to the hospital and after she was checked out by the medical staff he would interview her. Tamara really wasn't injured, other than a scraped elbow and a few broken fingernails when she tried to scratch her assailant. After a brief exam she was released and to her surprise, the police officer who responded to the 911 call had been replaced by Police Chief Ed Parker.

Chief Parker met her as soon as she left the Emergency Room and called her by name. She wasn't surprised to see him, because in a small-town police force with only six officers, the chief was very visible and responsive to the citizens. She was surprised that he called her by name. Tamara's greatest concern was for Drew. The chief told her he had some information about Drew and directed her to the far corner of the waiting room. As soon as she sat down the chief said, "Mr. Ashley's in surgery to relieve pressure on the brain. The doctor told him that the CT scan showed extensive swelling. I have the medical term right here. Just a sec."

Parker pulled a small pad out of his shirt pocket and read, "Ventriculostomy, that's the word. I guess this is a procedure where the surgeon drills a hole in the skull and inserts a plastic drain tube. The brain fluid is drained from inside the skull, helping to relieve the pressure. Sorry, I had to write it down because it was too medical for me. They also have to do surgery to repair his broken leg, but that may have to wait till a later day. He also has two cracked ribs but they don't require surgery. The surgeon said he will come out to the surgical waiting room when he is done, so if you're going to stay I suggest you go to that floor."

Tamara answered all the questions the chief asked. She had so little to go on since they were masked and attacked them from the bushes. She did tell him that one of the men, maybe the leader, said that Drew was "done for" and they took off running. The attack seemed well planned and the chief wanted to know about possible enemies. All Tamara could tell him was that Drew had lived in Manitou only a few months and seemed really well liked. She did ask the chief if he remembered the Williams family. Mr. Williams use to work at the paper mill and moved to Texas a number of years ago. The chief thought the name sounded familiar but he couldn't place them right off. Anyway, Tamara told him that Drew's deceased wife, Shelly, was the Williams' daughter.

She added that she didn't think there was any bad blood between them."

After taking a deep breath she told the chief about her house being burned and Drew's involvement with it. She also talked about the ongoing problems she was having with protests and the keying of her car. The chief said he had heard about the fire and knew that the school board was holding a special hearing. He wanted to know what was being done about the fire and when she told him that Detective Stedman was investigating the case but so far he hasn't got back with her. He rolled his eyes and said, "I'm going to check out his deceased wife's parents and also follow up with Stedman to see if he had any information.

The chief wanted to know if she had the names of family members so he could contact them. Tamara said that she didn't off hand but since she and Kathy were living in his apartment she would check his phone and see if she could find an address book or contact list. As the chief was getting ready to leave Tamara asked if he'd give her a lift home so she could change out of her jogging clothes and into street clothes. She wanted to be back at the hospital to talk with the surgeon when he was finished.

Chapter 16

As soon as the chief dropped her off Tamara rushed into Silent Sports to tell Kathy what had transpired. After telling Kathy all the details, Tamara told her she wanted to get back to the hospital as soon as possible. Kathy really tried to discourage it and Tamara was mildly surprised by her behavior. She responded by saying she couldn't believe that after all the things Drew had done for them she didn't want her to be by his side. Kathy tried to lessen her statement by saying she was concerned for Tamara's welfare, but it came across as ingenuine.

Since she was in a hurry to get back to the hospital, Tamara only did a cursory search for an address book or contact list. When she didn't find it right away she grabbed her wallet, cell phone and car keys and dashed out the door. Re-entering the hospital, she was much more aware of her surroundings than when she visited the E.R. She had lived in Manitou for a few years and had never visited the hospital before today. The two-story building was relatively new and in good condition. It was a regional hospital and seemed to be surprisingly well equipped. She just hoped the surgeons were as well equipped with the skills to match the hospital?

When she reached the surgical waiting room she was informed that the surgeon should be out to talk with her shortly. Sure enough, a doctor, who looked about Tamara's age, came out dressed in surgical garb and walked directly up to her since she was the only one in the waiting room. When he addressed her as Mrs. Ashley she had to correct him, which then alerted him to the potential HIPPA violations. He told her he was sorry and couldn't divulge any information.

Then, Tamara started crying and stretched the truth by saying they lived together and she was all he had. The doctor immediately assumed they were a couple and said, "Okay, without checking the approved contact list I can tell you this. The surgery to relieve the intracranial pressure was successful. The broken leg still requires surgery. However, the greatest threat to his health at this time is whether he suffered any brain damage and the fact that he is in a coma. We'll have a better idea after the swelling has gone down. Once he's out of recovery he'll be in the intensive care unit and you'll be able to see him for 10 minutes every hour. Sorry, I can't provide you with anything more reassuring."

While waiting in the intensive care waiting area Tamara started going through in her mind how she could contact Drew's mother. All of a sudden it occurred to her that her name would probably be listed in Shelly's obituary. Using her phone she searched the internet for a newspaper in Gloucester and came up with the Gloucester Daily Times. She decided to search first about Shelly's death and quickly an article came up that gave her the date. Then in a matter of minutes she had the obituaries loaded and searched for the day after the accident. The obituary came up and listed Shelly's family as well as a Barbara Ashley listed as mother-in-law. A white pages search for Barbara Ashley gave Tamara just the information she needed. There was a B. Ashley listed on Washington St.

Her hands were shaking as she dialed the number listed for Barbara Ashley. After three rings a woman answered and Tamara said, "I'm looking for Barbara Ashley the mother of Andrew." She used Andrew since she was not aware if his mother called him by his nick name. When the woman answered in the affirmative, Tamara continued in a very tentative manner, "Mrs. Ashley, my name is Tamara Elwell and I'm calling from Manitou, Michigan."

Before she could continue Barbara Ashley interrupted her by saying, "Tamara, why I know all about you. You're Drew's friend aren't you? You are the only person he has mentioned when he calls me and I can't tell you how happy that makes me."

Even though Tamara was shocked that she knew her name, she had to tell her about Drew. "Mrs. Ashley, Drew has been seriously injured and is in the hospital here."

From that point on Mrs. Ashley went into mother mode and her questions were delivered in rapid fire fashion. How come he didn't call me? How was he injured? Why did he need surgery? Is he going to survive? Who's the doctor and can I call him? When most of the questions were answered to her satisfaction, she said that she was catching a plane today and would make reservations as soon as they hung up. Tamara told her to fly into Traverse City or if not there Grand Rapids. She also told Mrs. Ashley to call her once she knew her flight and which airport and she or one of Drew's friends would pick her up.

The first ten-minute visit with Drew in the intensive care unit was horrible. Drew looked so sickly with one tube coming out of his bandaged head and another coming out of his nose. There was an IV stand with two bags dripping fluids into his arm and the digital equipment was flashing all kinds of numbers which gave the room an eerie appearance. The nurse checked him once while she was there and told Tamara to feel free to hold his hand and talk to him. She said no one ever knows what a person in a coma hears, but just to have a loved one near means a lot. There it was again. Another person assumed they were a couple. Taking the nurses advice she pulled her chair close to the bed and held his hand while talking softly to him about anything that came to mind.

Kathy checked in by phone every couple of hours and tried to get Tamara to come home. However, Tamara felt a sense of obligation to Drew. Since in her mind the reason he was seriously hurt was her fault and no way would she abandon him. Midafternoon Addie came running into the waiting room and immediately hugged Tamara. She was talking nonstop about how worried she was for Drew, and Tamara thought if anyone was observing Addie they would think that Drew was her husband. The fact that she was irritating Tamara was also easy for any observer to see.

Tamara's cell phone rang as they were both waiting for the next ten minute visit. She noticed on the caller I.D. that it was from Barbara Ashley. Mrs. Ashley first asked for an update on Drew's condition, which basically was unchanged from the first time they talked. She said, "I have my flight booked and I am almost at Logan. I couldn't get a direct flight to Traverse City or Grand Rapids but I was able to get a flight to Detroit and then transfer to a flight to Traverse City. I should be there at 8:00 tonight. Do you think you can meet me?"

Tamara was conflicted about what to do. If she left to pick up Mrs. Ashley, Addie would take over her place with Drew. If she asked Addie to go get Mrs. Ashley, then Addie would have all that time in the car building a relationship with Drew's mother. Why she was thinking these thoughts was beyond her. She took a risk and told her that Mike Edwards, Drew's contractor, would be there to pick her up. She asked for the flight number and arrival time and said she would see her tonight. Once they hung up she felt a sense of panic because she didn't have the slightest idea if Mike would be able or willing to get her.

A quick call to Kathy relieved some of her anxiety. Kathy had a great relationship with her cousin and said that she'd talk to him about picking up Drew's mother. Within a few minutes Kathy called back saying that everything was taken care off. Mike really liked Drew and didn't think twice about driving to Traverse to pick up his mother. Kathy also told her that she would take care of changing the sheets in their bed, so that Mrs. Ashley could sleep in it and they could sleep on the air mattress in the second bedroom. When Kathy asked if she was coming home soon, Tamara said that she would once his mother arrived. The silence on Kathy's end of the conversation was very telling.

Addie and Tamara went into his room for the 10 minute visit. He was still in a coma and showed no reactions even when Addie was kissing his cheek and calling him honey. Tamara was relieved when at the conclusion of the visit Addie said she had to get home to her daughter. However, once she left Tamara was alone with her own thoughts. Again she was very aware of having jealous feelings when Addie was around and yet she couldn't acknowledge that she wanted Drew.

Chapter 17

Before midnight, Drew's mother, an attractive middle aged woman, came into the waiting room accompanied by Mike. She immediately hugged Tamara as if they were long-time friends. Tamara started to call her Mrs. Ashley and she was quickly corrected to call her Barbara. Before Tamara could start again Kathy came into the room and hugged and kissed Tamara. Mrs. Ashley's eyes grew wide, but she quickly recovered as if she understood their relationship. Tamara introduced Kathy as her partner, so there was no doubt or at least she didn't' think there would be any doubt in Mrs. Ashley's mind.

Tamara started again from the beginning, "Barbara, Drew and I are friends and running buddies. We generally run together several times a week and usually run the same route at the same time. I have to tell you that I've been the target of severe harassment both verbally and physically. Drew literally saved me last week when our house was set on fire by these freaks. I don't think he'd have been hurt if he wasn't running with me. Three men attacked us when we were in a desolate area by the golf course. One of the men had a golf club and hit Drew numerous times on his head, chest and legs."

She continued, "I think they thought Drew was dead because one of them said," He's done for let's get out of here." I ran for help and fortunately a nurse lived in the house that was closest to us. I think she may be the reason Drew survived. As I told you earlier, the surgeon drained some fluid off the brain to relieve pressure. Drew also has some broken ribs but they don't present a problem at this time. They still have to do surgery on his broken tibia. The golf club caused a compound fracture and the surgeon told me that he'll most likely insert a rod to stabilize it. That surgery will probably occur tomorrow, whether or not Drew wakes from the coma."

Barbara couldn't wait to get into Drew's room, and upon seeing him, she broke into tears. Holding his hand, she kept saying, "Come on baby you're tough. You've handled lots of things worse than this. I need you to wake up." Then she just started telling stories about his childhood. "Remember that time you and Johnny thought you could fly and you both jumped off the garage roof. I thought you were dead, but you jumped up and said, 'I'll never do that again.' Or what about the time you went out on the tuna boat with Dad, and the hook went right through your hand. Dad said you didn't even cry when he pushed it through and clipped it off. Remember playing football your junior year when that huge kid from Saugus body slammed you into the ground. Everyone thought you were down for good but after a minute of lying there you got up and said is that all you've got. The next play you ran for a touchdown."

By the time ten minutes was up Tamara thought she'd heard all the stories of Drew's childhood. When they got back to the waiting room Kathy said, "Barbara, Tamara has been here since early morning and I think she needs to get home. I don't know if Drew told you, but we've been staying at his place till our apartment is finished. Anyway, I made up Drew's room for you if you want to come home with us."

Barbara thanked Kathy but said she planned to stay at the hospital overnight. She didn't want to miss a chance to talk with the doctor. Even though they both said the doctor wouldn't be back until morning Barbara didn't want to leave. She didn't miss a ten-minute visit but it didn't make a difference for Drew. He remained in a coma through the night.

Tamara was back at the hospital shortly after 7:00 the next morning. She found Barbara asleep in one of the waiting room chairs. As soon as she entered the room Barbara woke up and basically told Tamara there had been no change through the night. As they were talking a doctor entered the room. Tamara recognized him from yesterday and introduced him to Barbara. Then he told Barbara about the procedure he had done yesterday to relieve the pressure on the brain and what he had to do today.

He said that Drew was still in a coma which wasn't unusual considering his head had been used as a golf ball. His brain activity seemed within the normal range and the neurologist who did the consult felt that given time he would come out of the coma. The leg break was a different issue. The golf club caused a clean fracture of the tibia close to the ankle. The longer this break goes without being set the greater the risk that the ankle will not function properly. He told them he was planning on surgery this morning at which time Drew would still be administered a general anesthetic. He explained why they use a general anesthetic for comatose patients. "It is not just in case they are aware but more for hemodynamic stability". Recognizing they didn't understand him he said, "Hemodynamic control refers to a stable balance in the relationship between heart rate and blood pressure."

"Once in surgery," he said, "I'm going to use a procedure called intrameduallary rodding where I place a metal rod down the center of his tibia to hold the alignment of the bone. The surgical procedure lasts about an hour and a half, unless I find some other problem. Drew will have an incision over the knee joint, and small incisions below the knee and above the ankle. In addition, some fractures may require an incision near the break to realign the bones. I'll secure the IM rods within the bone by screws both above and below the fracture. The metal screws and the rod can be removed at a later date if they cause problems but can also be left in place for life. Tibia rodding provides excellent fixation and alignment of the bones, and he should fully recover the use of his leg. The most common risk of surgery is knee pain, and the most concerning complication is infection. If he gets an infection caused by the rod, it may require removal of the rod in order to cure the infection. But that's something we will face in the future, if it should ever happen."

They were back in the surgical waiting room and Tamara felt as if it was déjà vu. Things started to change about an hour into the surgery as friends started coming by the hospital. Mike and all his construction crew came by with a box of flowers that Tamara thought the boys must have arranged themselves because it was so ugly. When she received for the box she saw something sticking out between the flowers. There was a 4.5L bottle of Johnnie Walker Black Label. The boys all introduced themselves to Mrs. Ashley and told her stories about their many deck parties. The only one who stayed back from the group was Jimmy Hanson, and Tamara couldn't figure that out because he worked directly with Drew.

It was so obvious that he was avoiding them that Tamara approached him and asked to speak with him and led him to another part of the room. Tamara said, "What is your problem?"

Jimmy said, "I'm just doing what Detective Stedman said for me to do. You think I've done things to you and that I was there the night of the fire. The detective told me to keep my distance from you. Drew told him I was at the fire because he saw my truck. I told the detective I was nowhere near your house and would never do anything like that. I thought Drew was my friend and I was really hurt when he sicced the detective on me rather than talk to me himself. Besides I didn't even have my truck that night. I lent it to my brother Joe so he could get some hay for his horses."

Tamara was without words for a minute. She had struggled with her negative feelings about Jimmy and felt bad when Drew called her on prejudging him. Now she found out that Drew thought he was at the fire, and he didn't even tell her. At the same time Jimmy seemed genuinely hurt that Drew would accuse him of trying to burn her house down with her in it.

"I don't know what to think Jimmy," replied Tamara. "I'll be honest. I didn't trust you one bit and thought that the hatred your father felt for me carried through to you. It was Drew who told me I was being unfair to you, but still I never felt comfortable talking with you about the situation. All I can say is that I'm scared of what your father will do, and really what he's done. Our friend Drew is fighting for his life just because he befriended me. You sound convincing when you say you'd never do anything like that, but the only thing I've to go on is your father's actions."

"Tamara, believe me," said Jimmy. "I'm not my father and I don't hold his beliefs. I could tell you stories about the whippings I've received because I challenged his beliefs. There were times when he dragged me in front of the church and held what was called a "shaming lesson". The whole congregation surrounded me and started calling me names but it quickly turned to spitting on me and kicking me. Drew once asked me why I stayed in Manitou and all I could say was that it was my home. I don't mean my family but my friends. I heard from one of the church members that my father called a special council meeting and all the members left the meeting with fire in their eyes. I've no doubt that members of the church beat you and Drew but believe me I wasn't a part of it nor will I ever be a part of it."

The surgeon entered the room and called Mrs. Ashley and Tamara over to him and addressed them both. "I want you to know the surgery to repair the broken leg was successful. Of course he'll need physical therapy but based on Drew's overall health and age I expect a full recovery. You should be aware of the recovery time. I typically tell a patient it'll be a few months, even up to six months before he's running comfortably again. Hopefully there'll be no limp but it isn't unusual to see a slight limp in people with his injury. As far as the coma goes you'll need to talk with the neurologist, but I can tell you he didn't think there was any permanent brain damage. It may take a few days but he should come out of the coma. You'll have to wait till then before there can be any discussion about discharge. I'll check on him tomorrow. Before he is discharged I want to see him using the crutches. After that we can schedule a follow-up visit in my office in two weeks."

Mike and his crew left about as fast as they arrived. By their attire Tamara knew they were on their way to a job and Mike confirmed it when he told Tamara that if all goes well her apartment would be finished tomorrow. Barbara later asked, "Tammy, did I hear that man from the construction company correctly? He is working on an apartment for you? Is it an apartment in the building that Drew owns?"

Tamara replied, "Kathy and I leased the apartment a few weeks ago. It had nothing to do with the fire per se, although I was becoming very uncomfortable living in the country, particularly since I was the one receiving threatening phone calls and having my car keyed. With our store in the same building it only made sense. Wait till you see the apartments. Our apartment is a two-bedroom and matches Drew's but on opposite ends. Drew has really done an amazing job, not only with the apartments but with the whole building. I hope he told you about all the positive press he has received, and the big party the DDA threw for him."

Barbara smiled. "One thing about Drew is that he never bragged about things he was doing, but he did send me the newspaper story about the apartments. In Gloucester, he bought his first car wash the year he graduated from college and added a second a year later. They were always recognized as the best car washes on the North Shore. Tammy, it was very hard for him when Shelly died, and I have to believe his ending up here was not a coincidence. He was looking for something and I think he found it in this town and in you. I dreaded the day he left, because on top of losing a grandchild and daughter-in-law, I felt as if I was losing a son."

Tammy. No one ever called her by that nickname, and Barbara had used it two times in the last few minutes. Tamara was about to correct her, when all of a sudden it didn't make a difference. If it made her feel more comfortable, then she thought *I can handle her calling me that nickname*. They both waited quietly until it was time to visit Drew. He still looked terribly white, but on the positive side the tube from his skull had been removed. The nurse on duty greeted them cheerfully and said in no uncertain terms that it was time for them to go home. She reminded them that it would not help Drew if they become ill or worn out. She promised she'd call if Drew came out of his coma."

Tamara gave Barbara a brief tour of Manitou as they drove to the apartment. Before they went up to the apartment they stopped in Silent Sports to bring Kathy up to date. Barbara treated Kathy like an old friend and conversed as if they had known each other for ages. At one point Barbara referred to Tamara as Tammy, and Kathy almost choked holding back her laughter. Barbara asked if she had said something wrong and Kathy told her that Tamara usually attacks anyone that calls her Tammy. Barbara, in a motherly fashion, took Tamara's hand, and told her she thought Tammy was a beautiful name and used it because it fit her. Tamara laughed it off and told her okay, but she would be the only one allowed to call her that.

By the time they reached the apartment they were both dragging and too tired to even eat. Barbara took Drew's room and Tammy went into the second bedroom. She flopped on the air mattress and grabbed a pillow. When she laid her head on it she thought it smelled like Drew.

Amazingly, it acted like a sedative and within seconds she was in a deep sleep.

Chapter 18

Tamara only awoke from her sleep when she heard dishes clinking together as they were being taken out of the cabinets in the kitchen. When she walked into the kitchen she was surprised to see Kathy and Barbara preparing dinner. She was even more surprised to see that it was 6:00. She had slept over 8 hours. No wonder she felt so awake. Barbara said, "I just woke up myself and found Kathy starting to cook something for us to eat, which is very thoughtful. Tammy, I was wondering if you could drive me back to the hospital after we've had some supper."

Barbara was standing with her back to Kathy and didn't see the expression on her face. However, when Kathy responded in a taunting voice, "Yes Tammy, why don't you go back to the hospital too." Barbara felt like she had taken a jab from Kathy. Tamara wasn't surprised at the request but was surprised at Kathy's attitude. Kathy gave Tamara a stare that would freeze ice cubes and then said, "Don't you think you've spent enough time there. You have school in a little while and have so much to do before then. Also, Mike said that we can move in the day after tomorrow, and I know you wanted to shop for some household items. I just don't want you worn out."

Barbara tried to support Kathy and said that she was fine being there alone but Tamara wouldn't hear of it. The rest of the meal was very quiet. Kathy and Barbara did talk about Shelly. Barbara seemed to enjoy hearing stories about Shelly's early life. They talked a bit about Shelly's parents, and that seemed to open the door for Barbara to talk about her deceased husband. Barbara spoke in a quiet almost reverent tone. "Henry was a strong man who had a very clear moral compass. He was a near perfect husband who made me feel like a queen every day, and he would've been a wonderful father except he died too young."

"Henry's family settled Gloucester in the 1620's and for generations they were fishermen. When the haddock were fished out, they started fishing cod. Then the big container ships from Russia and Japan started sucking all the cod out of the North Atlantic. So he started fishing for tuna and that was lucrative for a few years. On his final trip a hook snagged him and pulled him into the cold North Atlantic Ocean. By the time the crew could reel in the line Henry had drowned. Drew was only four and never had a chance to really know his father. Because of the experience of losing my husband, I made Drew promise he wouldn't become a fisherman."

Everybody was quiet for a moment and then Tamara said, "You must've done a wonderful job because Drew's really a special person. His father would be proud of him." Again Kathy glared at Tamara but didn't say anything. Barbara replied, "I didn't do it alone. We had lots of family and friends that supported Drew and me. A couple of uncles made sure he stayed on the straight and narrow. They also helped me until I got back on my feet and found a good job at Gorton's Fisheries. I learned back then that nobody makes it through life on their own. You have to rely on others."

Later at the hospital, while sitting at Drew's bedside, the women were talking softly and Barbara was telling stories about Drew. Barbara talked about his childhood and Tamara talked about all the things he has accomplished in Manitou in only four months. Barbara was starting another story and said "Tammy." All of a sudden they heard a raspy voice say, "Who is Tammy and what is she doing in my room? Both women looked at Drew as his eyes were slowly opening and his cracked, dry lips broke into a smile. The women couldn't hold back and tears started dripping down their cheeks. Tamara pushed the call button and the charge nurse knew immediately what was going on the minute she entered the room.

After a check of all his physical indicators, Barbara and Tamara were permitted to return. The word they received was that considering what he'd been through he was in excellent shape. However, the nurse didn't want him to regress and still insisted on keeping the ten minute visit schedule at least for the remainder of the night. Tamara started to talk when Drew said, "How come she can call you 'Tammy', and how did she get here?"

Tamara replied, "She's the only person who has called me that name and gotten away with it. Maybe I was feeling sorry because her son was so beat up. But I'm warning you Buster, don't you try it." Drew chuckled and for the first time in a couple of days things seemed to be getting back to normal.

Barbara told Drew how Tammy searched the Gloucester paper to find her name and how she grabbed the first plane here. Tamara decided to let Barbara and Drew have some alone time and she was no sooner out the door when Barbara started in about her. "Drew, I know you're crazy about her but I don't know if she's the right one or even has the same feelings for you. I can deal with this same sex thing when it doesn't involve a member of my family, but now I just don't know. To me, it doesn't matter about their relationship, but I'm concerned about you. You've just started to recover from a terrible loss." Realizing that she was coming on too strong Barbara tried unsuccessfully to change the topic. "I have to tell you that what you have done with that building is amazing, and I can see that you've become an important figure in this city already. But I just have to say one last thing about Tamara and Kathy. I've had a chance to talk with both of them separately and there is no question they are a committed couple. All I can see is heartache for you. I didn't want you to fret over these matters right now."

Drew studied her face for a moment and could see the worry and strain reflected in her eyes. She had suffered through lots of trauma in her life too. First his father's tragic death, then Shelly and Bobby's death, and now his injury. He decided to reduce the stress in the conversation and simply said, "I'll think about what you said Mom."

Barbara decided to let Tamara go in by herself the next visit. Drew was getting very tired and they all agreed that this would be the last visit of the night. When Tamara walked to the bed he took her hand and asked if she was doing okay. He studied her reaction and immediately knew she was struggling to find words that expressed her feelings. Finally she said, "Drew, I feel so terrible for what's happened to you. You were almost killed because of me and I don't know what I would've done then. I'm at a point where I think there is no other choice for me than to leave Manitou. Who knows, after the school board meeting I probably won't have a job anyway."

Drew pulled her hand to his chest and said, "Look at me. You're not to blame for my injuries. There're some sick people in this town and we both know who's stirring them up. If you leave they win, and if they win the city of Manitou loses. You have to see this through, and I'm going to be there by your side. I'll be at the hospital for a few more days but I'll will be out before the hearing. Have you told Kathy what you just told me? Besides being life partners I thought you had a share in the business?"

"Listen Drew," Tamara said in no uncertain terms. "Kathy runs the business without me, and I don't have to be here for that. Her life has also been affected by the attacks on me, and just by being near her, I'm endangering her." Thinking about the text she read on Kathy's phone she added; "Besides I don't know what her plans are for the long term anyway."

There was no attempt to clarify her statement and Drew felt it was best to leave it alone for now. Whether Tamara and Kathy were having troubles was difficult to say, but it was evident there were some very active homophobes in this community. The physical assault on Drew was really attempted murder. They just didn't complete the task. The greater question was whether there were enough other people supportive of Tamara to swing the vote of the school board, He had nothing but time on his hands, and he thought *what better use of his time than to make lots of phone calls.*

Chapter 19

Meanwhile, just outside town, Jimmy Hanson parked his pick-up on a dirt two- track a couple of hundred yards from his father's church. He made his way through a wooded area and across a field until he could see the lights of the church. There were only six cars in the Living Spiritual Evangelical Church parking lot and he easily recognized the cars as owned by members of the church special council. His brother Joey's car was among the six. He could see lights on in his father's office but the rest of the building was dark. Jimmy had spent enough time around the church to know ways to get in without using any keys. The exterior door to the janitor's maintenance shop had never locked properly. All he had to do was to grab the door knob and lift up hard while pushing with his hip. The door popped open just like it always did.

In the dark janitor's room he could hear loud voices coming from down the hall. His father was on a rampage and that wasn't a pretty sight. He was talking about how they let God down. If they couldn't be God's soldiers who'd take up the sword? He was particularly mad at Joey, calling him a worthless idiot who couldn't follow the simplest plan. Speaking to all of them in military jargon, he accused them of aborting the raid on her house and not completing the goal of the ambush at the golf club. The police were going to be watching both of those sinners closely and also watching the members of this church. He reminded them that Detective Stedman told the council that both Elwell and Ashley made accusations about the church. "I don't want to risk anyone from here getting arrested. Your next chance to drive this aberrant whore from our community is at the school board meeting. I want to pack the meeting with members and friends of this church so that the board has no choice other than to relieve her from her duties. If that doesn't work, we'll just have to take it one step further."

Jimmy stayed hidden, waiting till everyone had left the church and then returned to his pickup the same way he got there. It was getting close to 11:00 when he drove past Drew's building and noticed the lights on in his apartment. Jimmy was never the most logical person, and even knowing that Drew was in a coma just yesterday, he assumed that with lights on in his apartment he must be home from the hospital. He walked up the stairs to the apartment level and knocked on Drew's door. Jimmy knew the door had a spy hole because he had installed it himself. He was just ready to knock again when the door flew open, and Kathy was standing there with a handgun aimed right in the middle of his chest. She looked prepared with her feet shoulder width apart and both hands steadying the weapon. Standing behind her like two sentries were Tamara and an older woman he remembered from the hospital.

Jimmy stammered, "What the fuck Kathy, I'm not here to hurt you. I need to talk with Drew. There are things I have to tell him that are important. Tamara, tell Kathy that I haven't done anything to hurt you or Drew. Tell her what I told you"

Kathy lowered the gun and said, "Get in here Jimmy. Knocking on our door at this hour scared the crap out of us. Drew is still in the hospital and we're all staying here for a couple of days. This is Drew's mother from Massachusetts, Mrs. Ashley. Now let's all sit down in the living room and you can tell us what's troubling you."

Drew told them everything that he'd overheard in the church. He told them that his father just about said they set the fires, and also attacked Drew and Tamara on their run. He said his father was mad because they didn't complete the job, and now his focus was on the school board meeting. He let them know his father was planning to pack the meeting with his supporters and pressure the board into firing Tamara. Finally, he looked at Tamara and said, "I'm really sorry for all the trouble they have given you. I also know now that my brother Joe is deeply involved in it. So I have to believe that the truck Drew saw at the fire was mine except I wasn't driving it, Joe was."

The three women stayed up talking for another couple of hours. A good part of the time they were problem solving how to care for Drew once he was released. The rest of the time they were trying to figure out a way to stop this crazy vendetta. They considered law enforcement and concluded they favored the city police over the sheriff's department. Tamara talked about the "icky" feeling she got during the interview with Detective Stedman. Chief Parker, on the other hand, didn't dismiss the situation as trivial and took Drew's brutal attack as a challenge to his police force.

Barbara was back at the hospital early the next morning. She drove Drew's jeep to the hospital because Tamara had to be at school early for a teacher's meeting. She felt she had developed a positive relationship with both Tamara and Kathy, and in all honesty didn't know if she'd given the right advice to Drew. She could see that Tamara was really conflicted, and it was very obvious this morning that Tamara was in emotional pain because she couldn't be at the hospital. Yet, she felt her advice to Drew was important

To Find What Was Lost

because he'd suffered enough and why open himself up for more possible pain?

Chapter 20

About 9:00, a distinguished looking man wearing a uniform entered Drew's hospital room. Barbara immediately stood up and waited while the man went to the bedside to greet Drew. He then turned and introduced himself as Chief Ed Parker of the Manitou Police Department. After some small talk he asked Barbara if he could talk with Drew alone. She gladly acquiesced, particularly if he was going to get to work on arresting the thugs who beat her son.

Drew wasn't able to give much help to the chief. He had little or no memory of the attack itself. Most of what he shared was information that Tamara had given him. He did have information about the raid on Tamara's house and told the Chief that he had shared that with the Sheriff's Detective. As much as he hated to point the finger at Jimmy, Drew told the Chief about Jimmy's pickup truck being at the house and his crashing into the side of it.

When the chief finished interviewing Drew, he met Barbara in the waiting room and suggested they get a cup of coffee. Barbara thought the Chief wanted to interview her, but when they got to the cafeteria he didn't seem to be asking those kinds of questions. Instead they talked about Boston and Gloucester and his almost going to Boston College on a football scholarship. Barbara talked about the fishing industry and how Gloucester, once the fishing capitol of the United States, had been undercut by the Russians and Japanese. She shared about her husband Henry drowning in a fishing accident and how it was a tough industry.

Barbara learned that Ed, she was now on a first name basis, was a widower. His wife of 30 years had died of cancer a couple of years ago. They each talked about how difficult it was to go on after losing a spouse. Ed shared that he thought once you lose a soul mate you'll never find another. He did feel his life was enriched by his three children and grandkids, and when he said that the tears started flowing. Barbara talked about only having one child and losing her only grandchild to a terrible accident. At that moment, they bonded in a way that only someone who has experienced loss could understand. They looked into the soul of the other and found refuge there.

Barbara did tell Chief Parker about their late night visit from Jimmy Hanson and his accusations about his father and members of the special council. She also told him that Jimmy swears he wasn't at the house the night of the fire, and that he'd loaned his truck to his older brother Joe. Although she didn't know Jimmy she told the chief that he sounded very convincing. As he was getting ready to leave the hospital, Chief Parker promised Barbara that he was going to bring the perpetrators to justice, and then he surprised her by asking if she would join him for dinner some night. Barbara stammered before saying yes and then gave him her cell phone number which was something she never did for anyone.

Back at the station, the chief started working on a plan. The first step was getting someone on the inside the Living Spirit Evangelical Church group. His officers were too well-known so he reached out to S.A.N.G. which stands for the Shoreline Area Narcotics Group. S.A.N.G. was supported by 15 different law enforcement departments in northern Michigan. The majority of its officers worked undercover and were experienced with the risks of going into dangerous situations.

The commander of the S.A.N.G. unit was a Colonel Tom Powers, a Michigan State Police Officer. Tom also happened to be a longtime friend of Chief Parker.

Colonel Powers took the phone call from Chief Parker as Ed knew he would. They had been friends long enough that they trusted one another, so that if one asked for help, they didn't question the other's motive. Chief Parker said that he needed someone unknown in his community to go undercover in a church. Furthermore, Parker explained that he thought the church was deeply involved in hate crimes. Parker added that just maybe there were some drugs being sold out of the church. He said it in a "wink, wink" fashion that Powers understood. By introducing the possibility of drug involvement Parker gave Colonel Powers the words he needed in case he was challenged by higher authorities for using resources in a Manitou church.

Powers said that he had just the person for the job and that this individual would benefit by staying in the shadows for a while. Manitou would be a perfect place for him. The colonel arranged for Chief Parker to meet this individual at the Panera Bread in Traverse City. He was reminded to wear street clothes and to drive his personal vehicle just in case someone from the drug community happened to be there. It was agreed that Chief Parker would just get a cup of coffee and sit in a booth. The undercover cop would find him.

Chapter 21

Things work fast in the drug enforcement area, and Chief Parker was scheduled to meet the undercover cop the next day at 10 am. For some reason meeting with the undercover officer wasn't the only thing on the chief's mind. He fingered the paper with Barbara's cell phone number and dialed before he lost the courage to call. Barbara answered after a couple of rings and also surprised herself when she accepted his invitation to dinner that evening. They agreed to meet at 6:30 pm at the Bunkers, a family style restaurant, located on the highway about three miles south of downtown.

Chief Parker and Barbara's dinner went better than either would have expected. There wasn't any discomfort and they talked like longtime friends without a lag in the conversation. Many of their interests were similar, even though they came from very different backgrounds They each loved Broadway musicals, but heard them in different venues. For Barbara it wasn't unusual to go to Boston and see a musical with the original cast before it hit Broadway. Ed, on the other hand, saw most of his musicals performed by high school kids, although he also attended many of the performances by the Civic Players and the community college located nearby. Ed tried to explain to Barbara that it wasn't about the quality but the spirit they put into their production. "I'll have to take you there so you'll understand."

They were at the table for three hours before they realized it, and neither wanted the night to end. Ed asked if she had walked the river walk yet and Barbara told him there hadn't been time. He said, "There is no way you can leave Manitou without walking the river walk, and tonight is just perfect for such a walk."

She followed him to a parking lot close to Drew's apartment and they both walked down to the wooden walkway that followed the river out to Lake Michigan for almost a mile. She was amazed how light it was for the time of night. They passed several small marinas and enjoyed watching the activity of the boaters as they relished the late summer evening. It wasn't planned and neither thought they initiated the idea, but before long they were walking hand and hand. Several times they passed people who acknowledged the chief, and Barbara could see that they were more interested in wondering who this stranger was holding the chief's hand than anything else.

Before leaving her at the apartment, Ed gently lifted her chin and tenderly kissed her lips. When Barbara entered the apartment she felt like a teenager who had stayed out past her curfew. Both Kathy and Tamara were sitting in the living room watching TV but she suspected they were more interested in where she had been the last few hours. All she had to say was that she had dinner with Chief Parker and the mood changed completely. Both Tamara and Kathy became like girlfriends saying, "Okay, you have to tell us everything."

Chief Parker was up early the next morning and at Jimmy's Juice & Java when they opened. He bought a large latte and egg panini before he headed out to Traverse City. It typically takes him about an hour and fifteen minutes to reach Traverse City, but today he gave himself plenty of time to think. He knew what he wanted the undercover officer to do and was planning in his mind how he was going to explain the duties, but his usually focused mind wasn't functioning at its best. Without trying, he was remembering the evening with

To Find What Was Lost

Barbara and realized that he hadn't felt that way in years. In the end his professionalism took over, and he had developed a workable plan by the time he reached Panera Bread.

Ed sat with his coffee trying not to look to conspicuous, but the harder he tried the more unnatural he behaved. Shortly after ten o'clock a man sat down across from him and stuck out his hand saying, "Ed?" The man looked like most twenty or thirty- year-olds in northern Michigan. He wore his hair somewhat long, had a few days growth of beard and wore a plaid shirt, blue jeans and work boots. In reality, he didn't look like a hippy or even a survivalist, because in northern Michigan if he said he was a college student or a scientist dressed as he was, you would've believed him. The best description was nondescript.

The chief spoke first and said, "Ed, Ed Parker. And you're who?"

The man smiled and said, "Josh Erickson. Pleased to make your acquaintance. I hear you may have some work for me?"

Chief Parker quickly went into cop mode and described the situation in Manitou. He talked about the civil rights violations and the illegal activities. He told Josh that he needed someone to get inside the Living Spirit Evangelical Church in order to confirm their involvement in the attempted murders and other charges. They concluded that it was best if no one knew that Josh was on the job including members of the Manitou Police Department or Manitou County Sheriff's Department.

After talking with Josh about some of his skills, they decided that his cover would be more effective if he had a job in Manitou. The Chief told him that he had a friend who owned a large sign company that had many employees and he could get him placed with that company. They decided that they wouldn't communicate directly but through Colonel Powers to prevent anyone from learning of Josh's infiltration into the church.

They agreed that the chief would call his friend and ask him for a favor. The chief would say that Josh was someone he arrested as a teenager and that he was trying to get on the right track. The owner of the sign company was a goodhearted person and always ready to reach out his hand to someone less fortunate than himself. All it took was one phone call and the job was set.

To Find What Was Lost

Chapter 22

Drew's recovery was progressing smoothly. Once he demonstrated to the physical therapist that he could manage the crutches, walk for a few hundred yards and climb a few stairs the hospital released him. Drew's excitement at being released was short-lived when he faced the stairs leading to his second floor apartment. He forgot that the street level stores had 20 foot tall ceilings which meant that he basically was climbing two flights of stairs. He was sweat covered by the time he reached the 2nd floor, and it made him wonder if his release from the hospital was premature.

The three women in his life were by his side the whole way. At first he thought that was great but he soon felt like he had three coaches giving him instructions. Thankfully, Tamara and Kathy had jobs and were not home during the day. His mother was a different story, and she was by his side every minute. On a positive note, he was surprised by her attitude, because he hadn't seen her so happy in years - or maybe ever. At first he thought it was because she was taking care of him and he was meeting her maternal needs, but one day he caught her laughing while talking on the phone. After some intense questioning, she told him that it was Chief Parker and that they had become friends.

Drew was shocked to learn his mother had a male friend, but it only took a second for him to realize how nice this was for her. He didn't know why she never dated when he was a child and hoped that it wasn't because of him. If she found a man she enjoyed being around then he was happy too. One afternoon while watching Dr. Phil together, he dropped a hint that if she wanted to invite Ed Parker to dinner it was fine with him. Little did he know that she would take him up on it so quickly and that same evening Ed would be at the apartment for dinner. For the first several days in September Ed, Tamara, Kathy and Ed's youngest daughter were frequent guests for dinner. The weather was still perfect and the evenings were ideal if you wore a light jacket for dessert on the deck.

Drew couldn't navigate the circular staircase to the rooftop deck but his mother and Ed and the others managed to go there most nights. Drew waited for an appropriate time and asked his mother directly about her relationship with Chief Parker. At first she acted offended and challenged him about checking up on her. She quickly realized that she was the one with the problem not Drew. He was asking a simple question and she went overboard with it.

She finally said, "Drew, I really haven't dated since your father died, and believe me I didn't think I missed it, but I really like this man. I like being with him and the way he makes me feel, and if you think you're going to get me into a discussion as to whether we've done it or not you are sadly mistaken. The reality is, I live over 700 miles away, and even though we're about the same age, he's a father with one daughter still in high school. Our lives are at such different places that it doesn't seem logical that our relationship will ever go anywhere."

Chief Parker did speak alone to both Tamara and Drew about his investigation and told them that he was making progress, but it'd take time. It was pretty evident that he trusted Tamara, and really had some good inside information about Tamara's relationship with the girls, since his youngest daughter was still on the cross-country team. His daughter was a strong supporter of Tamara and told him everything that went on during practices and in the locker room.

One of the most surprising occurrences happened because Ed invited Barbara to his house for dinner. That same night Kathy had made plans to meet a friend in Grand Rapids which left Tamara as the one to stay with Drew. At first he protested saying that he got around really well and didn't need a baby sitter, but that plea fell on deaf ears. Tamara stopped on the way back from school and picked up Chinese from the local buffet. She spread it out on the coffee table in the living room and opened some wine. At first it seemed like a typical dinner but then Drew stopped eating and just stared at Tamara.

Drew didn't say anything to her but reached for her hand. She allowed him to grasp it and moved closer to him as he gently pulled her. He took a finger and tenderly removed a piece of rice that was on her lip. With the rice on his finger he put it to his mouth in one of the most sensuous ways possible. Tamara was caught between emotions. She wanted to run, but the stronger urge was to grab hold of him. Drew, reacting to his own emotions, pulled her toward him as he lay on the sofa. She didn't back away or resist but instead fell into his arms.

The passion index skyrocketed from there, and in minutes they were tearing at each other's clothes. Drew unbuttoned the simple blouse she wore and unclasped her bra with ease. He had gotten into the habit of wearing jogging shorts and tees around the house and both items came off easily. It was his underwear that presented a problem because it caught on the cast and Tamara yanked them off in frustration. It was only afterward that she realized he could have been hurt. Drew didn't react at all and continued removing her shorts and underwear.

It may have been the forbidden fruit syndrome because the passion they both exhibited could have been recorded on the Richter Scale. Drew started kissing her head and breasts in a delicate manner. His lips surrounded her puffy nipples. Unlike Shelly who had full breasts, Tamara had the small, firm breasts of a runner, but to his mind they were perfect. It was at that point that he held her away from him and said, "Let's move to my bedroom." Part of this was so they could be comfortable, since his leg was in a cast, but the other reason was that the prophylactics were in his bedside table.

By now Drew could have told Tamara that he wanted to do it on the roof of her Willy's Jeepster and she would have complied. Once they hit the bed she mumbled something about being glad he had bought a new bed before he left the hospital. Drew took it, slow, making the foreplay feel like it would never end. Tamara reached a point where she demanded that he enter her and when he did she acted like she was in a firestorm. He tried to hold off as long as he could because she seemed to be having multiple orgasms. Finally, he could wait no longer and he came like never before. Drew collapsed on top of Tamara and just kept saying, "unbelievable, unbelievable."

They laid in bed with her head on his chest. They really didn't want to start a conversation but both knew they had to say something. Drew finally said, "I wasn't planning for this to happen, but I don't regret it at all and I hope you don't either?" Tamara was quiet for a moment and then replied, "That was amazing, and man, I couldn't believe how fast you had my bra off."

He chuckled and said, "Who would have thought that I still could do that after so many months with no practice. What are we going to do now?"

Tamara sighed and said, "I wasn't planning for it to happen either but I'm the one in a relationship. I have to deal with the consequences. It isn't as if I stopped loving Kathy yet at the same time I am really attracted to you."

Drew immediately said, "Stay with me. You can make that decision. One of the consequences can be that you and Kathy are no longer a couple. Tamara, I haven't felt like this in years, and I don't want to lose you."

They both heard the apartment door close and knew that Barbara was back. Tamara grabbed her clothes and quickly went into the bathroom. Barbara tapped on his door and asked if he was still awake. Drew told her to come in and as she did Tamara exited the bathroom. Tamara asked her how her night was and quickly excused herself saying that she had fed him, got him into bed and now had to clean up from supper.

Barbara looked at Tamara's flushed cheeks, the healthy glow on Drew's face and what looked like a sports bra in her hand and knew something other than feeding him Chinese food went on there tonight. She was a smart mother and didn't address her suspicions at all. In a few minutes Tamara reentered the bed room and said, "I've picked up the remains of our supper and think I'll head down the hall to our apartment. I'll see you tomorrow." She was out the door before either of them could say goodbye.

"So Mom," Drew started, "Why don't you tell me about your evening?"

Barbara cleared her throat and started in, "I had a wonderful time. Ed's house is very nice, and from the deck there is a view of Lake Michigan. It's been nice getting to know his youngest daughter, Cindy. She's the one on Tamara's cross country team and seems like a real nice girl. She didn't stay around long and right after supper went to her room to study. Ed's oldest daughter is a teacher and married to an engineer working with Ford. You know, the car company. The middle child is in college somewhere in Michigan."

Drew had to catch himself from smiling because his mother was talking so quickly it reminded him of the times he came in late and his mother questioned him. For some reason you always give out too much detail during those moments. The bottom line was that she was happy. She did surprise him the very next moment when she said, "I told Ed that I was going back to Gloucester the day after tomorrow. Maybe I'll come out for Thanksgiving if you'll have me. Right now, you can get around pretty well, and I've been away too long." In the back of his mind Drew was questioning whether she really felt she'd been away too long, or if she was getting attached to Ed and it scared her.

Drew had hit the nail on the head about Barbara talking too much. She was covering up the fact that Ed's daughter left shortly after she got there to spend the night with a friend.

To Find What Was Lost

By the end of the evening they were both in Ed's bedroom each smiling in nervous anticipation. Barbara told Ed as their kisses were becoming more passionate that she hadn't made love to anyone since her husband died. She was so worried that she'd disappoint him, but his gentle and reassuring manner soon had her relaxed. They slowly undressed each other and with each article of clothing her fears diminished and her confidence grew. At that very moment Barbara knew that she wanted Ed more than anything she had wanted in years.

Afterward lying in each other's arms Ed whispered, "You were amazing."

She smiled and said, "You were pretty amazing yourself. I guess I can say lovemaking is like riding a bike. Once you learn how, you never forget."

Chapter 23

Barbara Ashley gave Drew a big hug and kiss on the cheek and told him that she would be back really soon. He still required the crutch and leg cast but Drew's walking had improved a great deal, although navigating the stairs to the apartments was still an ordeal. He didn't have to worry about driving her to the airport because Chief Parker had already taken over that job. As the chief carried Barbara's suitcase down the stairs, Drew couldn't help but think they looked like two high school kids sneaking away. One quick glance over her shoulder with a quick wave to Drew and she was gone.

Drew immediately started calling names of families on lists that Kathy and Tamara had developed. He decided to start with the easy list first and called all current and former members of the Cross Country and Track teams. Most of the former members were no longer at home but it was their parents that he really wanted to talk with. Tamara was highly respected by the majority of the parents, and a number of them said they would attend the board meeting. The list of teachers' names was a partial success. Some of the teachers had their own cross to bear and wanted to use the board meeting as a time to address their issues. Other teachers were fearful of being targeted by the radical people who initiated the attack on Tamara.

Around 4:00 pm, Tamara entered the apartment and by that time he had called over 100 names and gotten a positive response from the majority of them. Tamara immediately came to the table where he was sitting and put her arms around him. She told him how grateful she was for everything he was doing about the hearing. With that she gave him a kiss and said she was going to her apartment for a shower. It was still a couple of hours before Kathy closed the shop, and this had become Drew and Tamara's special time. Drew immediately got up from his chair and invited Tamara into his shower because it had multiple shower heads.

She didn't resist and followed him into the master bath and waited while Drew adjusted the water. He left the bathroom and said to call if she needed anything. In anticipation that she might need something Drew covered the cast on his leg to make it waterproof. Just about the time he finished he heard Tamara call out, "Oh Drew, I need some help."

It didn't take him long to get into the bathroom. The large shower had caused the glass doors to steam over, but enough of Tamara's body showed through that it was a real tease. He pushed open the door and asked what she needed. Tamara turned toward him and said, "There are just some spots I can't get myself." Drew was in the shower with a bar of soap before she could say another word. He slowly started soaping her entire body, paying particular attention to the most sensitive body parts. Tamara's response to his touch was magnetic. The euphoria of the moment was intensified as the warm multiple spray heads stimulated their skin.

Drew stepped out of the shower and got a large super soft bath towel for Tamara. Again they enjoyed the experience of drying each other's body while stopping every so often for a kiss or hug. Tamara said, "I have to get back to the apartment and change before Kathy gets home. I don't know how much longer I can do this. I feel as if I'm leading a double life and yet I don't feel guilty. All I know is that when I'm with you I feel different. I was almost going to say "whole" but that would mean I don't feel whole when I'm with Kathy. I don't think that's fair to say either."

Drew said, "I have always told you how I feel about you. I want to be with you so badly that I've accepted this unusual arrangement, but I think we both know it can't go on this way. I want you Tamara, more than anything I've ever wanted in my life. Please remember that."

Tamara threw on the clothes she wore home from school, grabbed her bra, underwear and shoes and ran down the corridor to her apartment. She opened the door and there was Kathy standing in the kitchen. Kathy looked at her with her hair wet, and underwear in her hands and at first didn't comprehend what was going on. Then it hit her. "Oh my god," she cried, "You've been fucking Drew haven't you. I can't believe it. You kept telling me not to be jealous, and all that time I had every reason to be jealous. Well, aren't you going to say something?"

Tamara looked frozen in space but finally talked, 'It just happened Kathy. I didn't want it to, but it did. I love you and thought I'd never do anything to hurt you. I didn't plan to fall in love with Drew, but I have. I feel as if I should apologize, but if I did I'd only be apologizing for hurting your feelings. I can't apologize for what happened between Drew and me."

Kathy had tears running down her cheeks but it was difficult to tell if they were tears of sorrow or of anger. When she started speaking again it was clear that she was angry. "How could you do this to us? We were partners and pledged our love to each other. Who was there for you after your affair with the coach went bad? Who was there after the two guys raped you? It was me. I'm the one who comforted you and made things better. You were like a little wounded bird and I took you in and healed you."

"Who's Alexa?" asked Tamara.

"What?" said Kathy.

"You heard me. Who's Alexa?" said Tamara.

"She's a shoe rep. Why do you want to know?" asked Kathy

"In the middle of the night you received a text from her saying how much she missed you. I don't think that was shoe business I think you've been hooking up every time you left town on business. You try to sound so high and mighty but you're flawed too. Can you tell me that there's nothing going on between you and Alexa, or for that matter, any other women you've met on the show circuit?

After a brief silence Kathy said, "We have some work to do. Yes, I've messed around on you but it didn't mean anything. It was a simple hookup. What I see between you and Drew's much more serious. I see a relationship that goes deeper than just hooking up. I know you pretty well and don't think you entered into a relationship with Drew without a lot of forethought."

"You know Kathy, you're right. We do have lots of work to do," replied Tamara. "I'm just not sure that I'm interested in facing that challenge right now. And to be honest, the sentiment I felt from Alexa when I read her text was not just a simple hock up. Either you are not being honest with me or you have no idea what Alexa is feeling."

The rest of the evening was eerily quiet. Tamara spent most of the time in the bedroom and Kathy stayed in the living room. When Kathy was ready for bed she grabbed her pillow and a blanket and went to bed in the second bedroom. Through the quiet night the sobs of both women could be heard.
Neither knew if it was the end of their relationship, or just a bump in the road. Only time would tell.

That very same night Pastor Hanson called a special meeting of his congregation. He started with a prayer asking for God's wisdom and strength to deal with the sinful acts of people in the community. He then immediately started a 60-minute assault on gays, lesbians, cross- dressers and transsexuals. The people in attendance were getting pumped up, which was very similar to the way a coach fires up a team before the big game. During a break in the rhetoric, a booming voice from the rear of the church started yelling, "Pastor, Pastor, Leviticus 20:13 tells us if a man has sexual relations with a man as one does with a woman, both of them have done what is detestable. They are to be put to death; their blood will be on their own heads. Pastor wouldn't that also be true for two women."

Pastor Hanson didn't recognize the man but answered him by saying, "Our mission right now is to remove that sinful whore from our town, and we can do it through the school board." He then gave specific orders to those in attendance. A number of church members were to march outside the school building while holding signs with a variety of hate oriented statements such as, "Adam and Eve not Sandy and Eve", "Marriage is one woman, one man, no exceptions," "Heterosexual Pride", and "Celebrate diversity, marry someone of the opposite gender".

The remainder of the people were to fill as many of the front seats of the meeting room as possible. The Pastor encouraged people to call like-minded friends and get them to come to the hearing. He then said that at an appropriate time he'd give a signal and in unison they were to stand and start chanting "God hates Fags. Fear God not Fags". As the meeting was coming to an end Pastor Hanson leaned over to one of his special council and asked him to bring the man quoting the Bible verse to him.

Josh hoped that he'd spoken strong enough to get the pastor's attention, and he was particularly aware of his dress. He wore a clean plaid shirt and denim pants, and on his head was a ball cap saying, "Pro God, Pro Life, and Pro Guns". Having been undercover in a couple of situations he knew he had to look similar to the other members, but not so similar that it looked phony. He had his hair cut that morning into a military cut. The overall appearance was of a working man who took care of himself and for all accounts god-fearing.

When the man tapped Josh on his shoulder, it didn't surprise him. The man walked him over to the office and opened the door. The Pastor and several other men were standing there. Pastor Hanson immediately reached out his hand and said, "I haven't had the pleasure of being introduced. I'm Ralph Hanson, Pastor of this church. And you are?"

Josh gave his name as Jack Thompson, and at first only provided a little bit of personal information. He wanted them to dig a little so that it appeared like the natural way a stranger with his views would react. He eventually shared that he had just came to town and was working for the local sign company. He let it be known that his ex-wife had run off, and when he went to get her back he was slapped with a restraining order. The second time he tried to get to her he was held in the county jail for a couple of months. He told them he had since lost his job and truck because of that slut he married but knew better than to stay near her so he moved to Manitou.

The pastor stared at Josh for a long time and then asked, "Mr. Thompson, will you be able to stay for our brief meeting. I think you could be a help to us." He didn't wait for a reply and just assumed that his invitation was really an order. Josh gave the impression that he'd be really happy to help in any way.

The meeting was actually brief and its only purpose was assigning duties to the special council members. Just as they were about to leave, Detective Stedman spoke up. "Pastor, I've done some digging and found something that may interest you. I think it would be a big help at the hearing."

Pastor Hanson said, "Well, God needs all the help he can get. So what's this information?"

Stedman continued, "I did some digging into Elwell's background and found nothing at all. I was just about to give up when I stumbled upon something that was incongruent with the rest of her history. She quit track before her senior year at State and gave up her scholarship. She didn't quit school and there was no injury. Now why, I ask myself, would a young woman give up a scholarship worth thousands of dollars? I did more digging and found a janitor who was in charge of the locker room and varsity exercise facilities. He told me he heard she had sex with two male members of the track team and the coach caught her. He never heard another thing about it and just assumed they cut a deal with her to just quit the team and give back the scholarship."

The pastor was getting very excited the longer Stedman spoke, and finally he clapped his hands and raised them toward the ceiling. He started speaking in preacher fashion saying, "God has heard our prayers and is showing us a path to take. This is just the kind of information we need to take to the school board hearing. It clearly shows her character. Can you get him here for the hearing?"

Stedman shook his head and said, "He won't come and probably wouldn't be a good witness. I think for the purpose of the hearing I can give a report that reveals my findings. It should carry a lot of weight. The board is already nervous about having a known lesbian on their staff, and this'll put them over the edge."

To an outside observer one would've thought that these men had won the lottery. They left the church smiling, slapping each other on the back and eager to attend that special board meeting. Josh seemed to have succeeded in at least being accepted into the group. As he walked out, a couple of the men asked if he was interested in subbing on their bowling team and another asked if he was interested in the Eagles Club. The coup de gras for winning over the men was when Josh jumped on to his Harley Road King and kicked gravel leaving the lot.

After the council had left the office Pastor Hanson picked up his phone and called a local number. After a few rings, someone answered, and the pastor said, "Mrs. Mueller, this here is Pastor Ralph Hanson. Do you have a few minutes this evening when I can talk with you and your husband? I know it's late but I think it's important."

Pastor Hanson arrived at their door within fifteen minutes. When they were all seated in the living room he said, "I know you folks have been worried about your daughter. I've seen you in our church a couple of times and that's God's way of telling me that you're looking for answers. Well, I think I've some answers for you. I have proof that your daughter is a victim, and her partner has tricked her into a salacious relationship."

He went on to explain how Tamara Elwell was an evil person sent by the devil to corrupt their daughter. He told them about her seducing two college boys and then being kicked off the track team because of her behavior. The Muellers listened to him with interest, and when all was said and done, agreed to attend the school board meeting and sit with the people opposed to Tamara Elwell remaining as a teacher in Manitou High School.

Chapter 24

The hearing was scheduled to take place in two days, which put pressure on Drew if he was going to finish making the phone calls. He again asked Kathy and Tamara for a list of any other people that would be supportive of her as character witnesses. The list, like the first that Tamara provided, was mainly members of the Blue State track team and a few people she knew from town. She also had several teachers listed as friends who would speak on her behalf. Drew made two columns. One was for people who would attend the hearing and the other was for people willing to be character witnesses. It took a few hours, but in the end he had four people ready to speak as character witnesses and twenty-five coming to the hearing to give her support.

The one thing that had been bugging him since he first became friends with Tamara was her relationship with her parents. She talked about her happy childhood and how open and accepting her parents were when she was living at home. It was hard for Drew to fathom how these so-called liberals could switch so dramatically when they found out she was in a lesbian relationship. He knew there was only one way to find out the answer and that was to contact them.

It didn't take him long to locate her parents. There were only two Elwell's in Flint and the other was an eighty year old man. He didn't want to call them because they didn't know him, and this was such a personal matter he wanted face to face communication. He checked with Google Maps and learned Flint was only a little over three hours away. With his leg in a cast he still couldn't drive a stick shift so the next best thing was recruiting a driver. Bingo! Jimmy Hanson was his man, and for a little money he was sure Jimmy would drive him there.

Drew didn't tell anyone where he was going because if it didn't work out he didn't want to hurt Tamara's feelings. He even turned off his cell phone fearing that if Tamara called he would blurt out where he was going. Jimmy drove Drew's Wrangler and they arrived in Flint a little after five. Using his GPS system, he had no trouble finding Tamara's parents' home. As she had described, their home was in a very nice area of Flint. For many people that may sound like an oxymoron, but in reality, it was a beautiful neighborhood of older, well-kept homes in the same city that was known for poisoned drinking water and abandoned homes. The Elwell's house looked like the type of home Beaver Cleaver would have lived in. As he pulled up to the house there were kids playing on the street, and Drew thought to himself *this is a great neighborhood* before even stepping out of the car.

Jimmy stayed in the car as Drew made his way to the front door. Since it was after work hours, his whole plan counted on someone being home. He rang the doorbell, and in a few minutes it was answered by a young guy who looked in his late teens or early twenties. Drew asked if this was the Elwell residence, and when the kid responded in the positive, Drew asked if Mr. or Mrs. Elwell was home. Wanting to create a good atmosphere he reached out his hand and said, "My name is Drew Ashley and I really would like to speak to the Elwells."

At that point the young guy took his hand and said, "I'm Austin, their son. Give me a minute and I'll find them. Why don't you step inside?" Austin disappeared and Drew stepped into the foyer. There was no hesitancy on Austin's part in inviting a stranger into his home. Drew couldn't see any family resemblance between Austin and Tamara, but that didn't surprise him. The house was a center stairway colonial and he could see that it was well cared for.

It didn't take long for an attractive woman who looked a lot like Tamara to come to the foyer. She immediately introduced herself as Pat Elwell and asked if she could help him. This was the moment Drew was most uncomfortable with. How he phrased his next sentences meant everything, so he spoke softly and slowly. "My name is Drew Ashley, and I drove down from Manitou in order to talk with you and your husband. Is he home?"

Pat stared at him and looked a little ill at ease. "He should be home any minute. Is there something I can help you with? Is this about Tamara? Is she okay?" Austin was standing back and could tell his mother wasn't comfortable so he asked her if everything was okay.

Drew smiled as he tried to make her feel at ease and said, "I'd really like to talk to you both at the same time, and I can wait in my car till he gets here."

At that point Pat recognized there was no reason to be fearful and invited Drew into their family room. The room at the back of the house was glass from floor to ceiling and gave a beautiful view of the huge oak trees throughout the neighborhood. Drew did share that he wanted to talk about her daughter but thought it was best to tell everything at once. With that information, she asked if he wanted a soft drink and teased him a bit by promising not to give him Flint water. He laughed and then said "no", leaving them to sit and watch the wall clock tick off the minutes.

It wasn't very long before Drew saw a car pull into the driveway and he assumed it was Mr. Elwell's. Pat Elwell got up and went to the back door where Drew was certain she was filling him in on their strange visitor. Mr. Elwell entered the room and Drew could see he possessed the same runner's physique as Tamara. He was tall and lanky and looked like he could run a marathon any day of the week. He immediately approached Drew and introduced himself as Carl Elwell.

He was a man of few words and quickly stated, "What's this about?"

Drew suggested they all sit down, including Austin, and then he started. "I don't know how much Tamara has told you about her situation in Manitou, but it is very serious. She is facing the worst kind of sexual harassment, and it has reached a dangerous point." The Elwell's were obviously unaware of what was happening and both tried to get the answer at the same time. It took a few seconds to get them calmed down.

Drew continued, "I moved to Manitou from Massachusetts four or five months ago and immediately developed a friendship with Tamara and Kathy. Tamara and I started running together and she shared some of the harassment she has faced. Her car has been keyed a couple of times with terrible words written on it. A few weeks ago a group of men surrounded the house she and Kathy were living in and set it on fire. She called me in a panic, and I had to break out the back window to pull her out of the house. Two weeks ago, we were running together when three men tackled us and beat me with a golf club. They left when they thought I was dead. Finally, the school board is holding a special hearing to determine whether Tamara should remain on staff due to her moral character."

By this point both the parents were getting alarmed and asking so many questions that Drew couldn't respond fast enough. He finally got them quiet and said, "Tamara doesn't know I'm here and she'd kill me if she knew. She has a lot of pride and probably would've asked for your help, but she also said that things haven't been the same between you since she started a relationship with Kathy. What I'm here to tell you is that she needs you more than ever. The hearing is the day after tomorrow, and if there's any way you can be there to give her support, it'd be unbelievable."

Carl Elwell asked, "What's your relationship with Tamara?"

Drew replied, "Great question. She and Kathy are now renting a two bedroom apartment in the building I own. But I wouldn't be honest if I didn't tell you I love your daughter. Things are very complicated. She is struggling with multiple issues but I think she feels something for me too. However, I know she loves Kathy, and I'd be upset if my sharing how I feel about her caused you to put pressure on Tamara about her relationship with Kathy."

Pat responded first, "We'd never do that. We just want our children happy, and that means that falling love with the right person is really what matters. We think Kathy's a great girl, but we're never invited to visit them, and they don't come here. So I think Tamara has control of that part of our relationship. We never knew what happened at Blue Water State and why she quit the track team, but from that point on she has really avoided us, and I mean all of us, including her brothers Austin and John."

"What do you think she needs? All we know is that she cut us out of her life, and to be honest, we all were very hurt. It's really hard when one of your children stop relating to you and you don't know why." said Carl.

"She has shared some things with me that I can't divulge, but I really think she needs you. She talks so positively about your family but has let this relationship with Kathy come between you. Give her your love and let her know you support her and see where it goes from there. I'm in the same boat as you. I know what I want in terms of our relationship, but I don't know what she wants."

After discussing details of the hearing, Drew said that he'd better get on the road before it was too late. Pat told him, "You have to have something to eat. We were all heading to Angelo's Coney Island for a quick supper. Why don't you join us? It won't take long and you have to eat something tonight."

Drew agreed once he told them that his driver, Jimmy, would need to come too. He found out that Angelo's Coney Island is a Flint landmark. It's the kind of place found in every city where former residents and college kids returning home have to go to or else it isn't a visit home. Drew had to agree with them that the chili dogs and onion rings were great. Jimmy seemed to hit it off with Austin which allowed the

To Find What Was Lost

Elwell's and Drew plenty of chance to talk about a variety of issues. Before they left Angelo's Drew had told them the whole story of why he ended up in Manitou. They learned about Shelly and Bobby and his year of being super depressed. When he was talking about Shelly, Pat reached over and held his hand and Drew could see the tears forming in her eyes.

As he said goodbye Drew felt he had met some new friends. They seemed like genuine people, the kind of folks that he wanted to be around. It also gave him a better understanding about Tamara. It seems that they weren't reacting to her choice of sexual partners as much as she was. He also remembered that she never shared about her love affair with the coach or being raped with her parents and that he found unusual. All he could think was that Tamara had so much pride that she didn't want to let her parents down and chose to suffer alone.

Chapter 25

The hearing was the next night and Drew didn't know of anything else he could do to help Tamara. He still was unsure if her parents were going to be at the hearing, although they seemed fairly certain they'd be there. He hadn't heard anything from Kathy or Tamara as far as additional people to call or other things he could be doing. The last he saw of Tamara, she was hustling down the hallway with her hair wet and underwear bundled in front of her.

At the same time Tamara wanted so much to talk with Drew and to feel him embrace her, but she was also pissed because he disappeared on her and was unavailable to comfort her, particularly after the terrible argument she had with Kathy. It bothered her that she couldn't get in touch with him yesterday afternoon and evening, and she really questioned why his cell phone wasn't in service. He'd shut it off for some reason.

Her established running routine changed completely. She didn't feel safe running alone and Drew wouldn't be able to run for months. Kathy had run with her a few times, but since their argument they hadn't talked. Three girls from her cross-country team were thrilled when she asked them to run with her but that meant the running would be late afternoon, and she was typically an early morning runner. Running in the afternoon also meant she wouldn't see Drew till dinner time and she realized that disappointed her. In fact, what became very clear to her was that she was thinking more about Drew than Kathy.

She had to get through the next couple of days and hopefully if the hearing went well, everything would start to settle down. It was difficult going to school and thinking that everyone was talking about you. A few of her closer friends tried to make light of it, but no matter how one looks at it, the hearing was serious business.

Chief Parker was sitting at his desk trying to develop a game plan for tomorrow evening's hearing. His friend, Col. Powers, had talked to him yesterday and informed him that Josh Erickson had learned the part of the Pastor's plan where he planned to attack her moral character. There wasn't much the Chief could do about the report of Tamara's past sexual behavior. In the short time he had known Tamara, he never got the impression that she was an amoral person, and he was a good judge of people. About the only thing he could do was to alert Tamara and Drew about the surprise the Pastor was planning on introducing at the meeting. Thanks to Josh, the chief knew that Stedman from the sheriff's office was a member of the pastor's council and potentially a dangerous man.

The chief's phone rang and it was the front desk saying that he had a visitor from the FBI. He told the officer that he would be down to meet her, but when he got there he didn't spot an agent. The only person in the waiting area was a high school or college student sitting expectedly on the wooden bench. Before the chief could ask the officer about the agent, the so-called student rose from the bench and said, "Chief Parker?"

She then reached out her hand and introduced herself as Agent Stephanie Willis. She looked a little older up close but still could pass for a teenager if she had to. Agent Willis was very attractive, with long blond hair, and even her business suit couldn't hide her shapely body. After she declined the obligatory cup of coffee the chief walked her back to his office.

She began to talk once they were seated. "Chief, I'm stationed in the Indianapolis Field office and currently in the Fraud Division. Last week you did a record search on a Reverend Ralph Hanson. Would you mind sharing what you were looking for and how long you have known him?"

The Chief replied, "I'll be glad to if you share with me why you are interested in him." She nodded an affirmative with her head so he continued, "Pastor Hanson moved into our community a few years ago. He bought an old commercial building and renamed it The Living Spirit Evangelical Church. The congregation has grown rapidly, with the majority of its members being older blue-collar folks. Don't get me wrong. There are younger folks too but the majority of them are hardworking people who see themselves losing ground and don't know what to expect in their future."

"The pastor seems to prey on them by giving sermons which place the blame for all the problems on gays, immigrants, abortionist and the like." He always has a group carrying signs that express outrage on all the issues. Although I haven't got the proof yet I'm close to getting enough on him so that I can arrest him for organizing a physical assault as well as arson. I also think there is a case for violating civil rights that the FBI could act on. An undercover officer from the Shoreline Area Narcotics Group has been loaned to me and he has infiltrated the pastor's special council."

To Find What Was Lost

Agent Willis stopped writing and said, "I guess it's now my turn. As I said I'm with the Indianapolis Regional Office, which covers all of Indiana. Ralph Hanson came to our attention the first time about ten years ago which was long before I joined the agency. He had a storefront church in Indy, and although we had some complaints about the hatred he was preaching, our greater concern was fraud. He had several older members turn over their life savings to him with the understanding that he'd take care of them for the rest of their lives. He left that church and those senior citizens high and dry. They didn't file a complaint because they either died, were too embarrassed or still believed in him. We only heard about it through a couple of their children, but there was no way to build a case against him."

"About four years ago he was doing the same thing in Fort Wayne. He seems to choose an area where there are lots of disadvantaged whites and earns their support by identifying how blacks, Hispanics, gays and lesbians have taken everything from them. Issues like abortion and same sex marriage just adds fuel to the fire. Again he seemed to convince some seniors to give him their life savings. He was also using the tax-exempt status of the church to do many questionable financial deals. One thing he did was to purchase large ticket items and divert the items to cash for himself. Last but not least, his wife disappeared while they were living in Fort Wayne. He never filed a missing person complaint and she hasn't turned up anywhere. However, there were several people talking about how she ran away from him and didn't want to be found."

The chief responded, "I haven't heard of any complaints about defrauding senior citizens but I'll mention it to my man on the inside and see what he finds. It's interesting that you mention disadvantaged whites because, as I told you that seems to make up his congregation here. There are some exceptions and they seem to be in the leadership council. What I've been dealing with is direct attacks on two young women living together. They are a couple and make no effort to conceal it. One of the women grew up here and for some reason she isn't the primary target of the attacks. The other woman is a teacher and coach. Her car has been keyed on two occasions, and the words are clearly anti-gay. Her house was surrounded by men in masks, a cross burned in the lawn and the front and back doors blocked by bales of hay that were set on fire. A man who's her friend busted out a window and saved her."

"The most recent incident is a case of attempted murder. The woman who has been harassed was running regularly with the gentleman friend and they were attacked while on a run. She only got a few bruises but the man had his skull smashed in with a golf club and suffered a compound fracture of his tibia. Thanks to the quick response by a nurse living in the neighborhood, and the EMT, he survived but did require brain surgery. His leg will take months to be right again. We know members of the special council were involved, but the proof is all hearsay. I'll put you in touch with the undercover officer and he may have some way to get information on fraud or diverting funds from the church to his person."

Agent Willis asked for the names, addresses and contact numbers for the two women being harassed and the man who was beaten. She told the chief that it wouldn't hurt for the FBI to look into the current matter since she was here to follow up on the case. The FBI was very involved in civil rights cases, and a crime toward someone because of their sexual orientation was a high priority. She said goodbye and told the chief she would be in touch with him.

About 4:00 pm Drew decided to call Chief Parker to see if he had any additional information and if there were any suspected problems for the night of the hearing. The chief said that he had three officers on duty at the school and had contacted the sheriff just in case they needed back up. In the course of the conversation the chief mentioned that a source had told him that they had information about some sexual indiscretions of Tamara when she was in college. The chief asked Drew if he was aware of anything that could come up. Drew didn't know how to answer at first and then decided to tell the chief a version of the truth. He said that something happened to Tamara while she was in college but he didn't know all the facts. The chief accepted him at his word and told him he would see him at the hearing. Just before he hung up the Chief said, "It was good your mother got home without any complications. You know how flying is these … days."

Drew was sitting in his living room trying to come to terms with the idea that his mother and the Chief have continued to be in communication when there was a knock on the door. Tamara stood there looking forlorn and said, "Where have you been? I called several times last night and it went directly to voice mail."

Drew took her hand and with very little effort pulled her into his arms. "I'm sorry if I wasn't available but I had some personal business that had to be taken care of. By the time I got home last night it was really late and I didn't want to bother you."

She continued, "When I walked into our apartment yesterday after our little tryst in the shower Kathy was there. We had a huge blow up. It was terrible. She said things and I said things that we may never be able to take back. I told her that you and I have made love and that I have feelings for you. At the same time I suspected she was cheating on me and accused her of it. After some really hostile exchanges she admitted to hooking up with people when she is out of town. She seemed surprised that it would bother me and tried to justify it by saying they didn't mean anything to her whereas you mean something to me. I couldn't argue with her on that point and we ended up sleeping in separate rooms. It sure is nice having a two bedroom apartment"

"Where do things stand now?" Drew Asked.

"We haven't talked since then and it may be a while till we figure things out. I know I sound selfish but I don't want to lose you and yet I still have feelings for Kathy. I've got to clear my mind to get ready for tomorrow. Do you think you can offer a girl some wine?"

First, there was wine and then they ordered pizza and before 7:00 they were in Drew's bed. Their lovemaking had a sort of intensity to it that reflected both of their feelings. Obviously the hearing and the issue with Kathy was on their minds. They held each other for hours and when both felt satiated they drifted off to sleep. Tamara woke up at 11:00 p.m. and told Drew that she was going back to her own bed. They separated with a kiss and both were questioning whether this was their last kiss.

Chapter 26

The day of the hearing didn't start like any other day. Drew was enjoying a cup of coffee when his phone rang. Kathy was on the line and said she wanted to know if he was up because she needed to talk with him. Drew had no idea what to expect, and he got very anxious waiting for Kathy to walk down to his apartment. He knew that it wouldn't be a pleasant discussion once he saw her face. She was furious with Drew and her blood pressure was probably close to boiling.

She didn't wait till they were seated before she started in, "You stabbed me in the back. I thought we were friends, but no you had to do things to win Tamara's affection. There used to be a time when people could sue for alienation of affection. Yes, you were the nice guy who was always ready to give Tamara a shoulder to cry on. You rescue her from a burning house, offer her shelter, run with her every day and even risk your life for her, but then you take her to bed. You must've known how fragile she is and how easy it'd be to sway her affection. You're no better that a snake preying on an unsuspecting victim."

Drew had heard enough and interrupted her saying, "Tamara told me all about what happened at Blue Water State and how you were there to help her pick up the pieces. Don't you think you were targeting a girl who was in a fragile position then? You took her in to rescue her and, what a surprise she ends up in your bed. Tamara fell in love with you then and trusted your advice. She relied on only you and didn't fight back for some reason. She didn't file rape charges or charges against the coach. She gave up her scholarship, track team and, in reality, gave up her parents. Before you start calling me names, why don't you take a look at yourself. I'm in love and want to be with Tamara, but she'll be the one that decides between us. I'm not backing down."

Kathy slammed the door as she left the apartment. Things were coming unraveled for her. She knew that Tamara was taking a lot of abuse and recognized that she could have been seriously injured or killed. At the same time she believed if Tamara would just hold her ground this whole thing would blow over. She didn't believe that Pastor Hanson, a newcomer to town, would have enough influence to drive Tamara from her school job. She was stunned by Drew's accusations that she provided a safe harbor for Tamara as a ploy for getting her into her bed. Kathy had no use for Tamara's parents and their so-called liberal attitudes. They didn't fight for her and were too comfortable accepting her weak reason for quitting track. A parent who really cared would've seen through that flimsy excuse. Kathy also couldn't accept that Tamara was pissed because she hooked up a few times. Besides Tamara had been like a cold fish over the past several months and Kathy had always needed more physical loving than Tamara.

There was electricity in the air the night of the hearing. The TV stations from Grand Rapids, Traverse City and Cadillac were there with their satellite towers in the air. The outside of the school was crowded with people picketing and holding signs. Most of the signs seemed to be against Tamara, but there were pockets of supporters. Drew arranged for Jimmy to meet them at the front door so he could park the Car while Drew walked Tamara to the meeting. At first, Jimmy didn't recognize the car until he saw Drew who quickly explained that with a walking cast he needed to rent and automatic in order to drive. Drew tried to tease Jimmy by saying it also was a good time to have the Jeep in a bump shop to get rid of the red paint and dent.

The hundred foot walk from where they exited the car to the front doors of the school felt like a mile. Angry, vile people lined the walkway yelling at Tamara and holding signs that couldn't be repeated on most media. The pastor had done his job and got the crowds out to protest. A couple of Manitou Police were standing at the front door, not allowing anyone carrying signs to enter. Someone from the school administration was telling the police how many more people could enter the auditorium. The meetings were usually held in the library, but this special hearing was moved to the auditorium where the atmosphere was more like a sporting event or a concert.

The place was packed, and when Tamara entered the auditorium there were cheers and boos. The way the people were reacting one would've thought that Jerry Springer's audience had come to Manitou. The crowd wasn't here for educational purposes. They wanted entertainment. The stage was set up so the school board members were sitting behind two tables arranged in a V-shape facing the audience. The superintendent sat at the end of the table. The front row of the auditorium was kept open for Tamara and the union representative.

Drew walked her down the aisle then said that some friends had saved him a seat behind her in the second row. She turned and saw her mother and father for the first time. She reached over the seats and hugged them both as tears were streaming down all their faces. Pat Elwell said, "Why didn't you tell us what was going on? We would've been here in a minute to support you. We'd never have known if Drew hadn't driven to Flint yesterday and told us."

Tamara was struck with mixed emotions as she looked at Drew. She didn't want her parents to know the mess she was in, and she was mad at Drew for assuming she needed her parents. On the other hand she needed her parents more than ever before and she couldn't believe Drew would go to such extremes to help her. All she could say to them was they'd talk after the hearing.

The school board president slammed his gavel down several times before the room quieted. In their typical fashion they started the meeting with the pledge of allegiance. He then stated that this meeting was called for the single purpose of considering allegations against Tamara Elwell, stating that she's morally unfit to be a teacher. He said that he'd read the formal complaint filed by two parents, after which the board would hear comments from the floor followed by comments from Ms. Elwell. He added that Ms. Elwell had chosen not to have legal counsel at the hearing although she is accompanied by a representative from the teacher's union. Finally, he added that Ms. Elwell has been a teacher in the district for almost three years and her previous evaluations have classified her as highly effective.

The two parents read their written complaints, and it was very difficult for Tamara to hear their comments. Tamara thought she had a good relationship with the girls of these parents. In both cases it was the fathers who read the complaints. The mothers stood next to them with their heads

looking down. When the president opened the meeting for public comments a number of people lined up to speak. It was clear the church had many people primed to talk. Some parents were charging her with trying to turn their daughters into lesbians.
Others complained that she stares at the girls while they are taking showers.

However, Drew had done a good job of getting parents and teachers to the meeting, and as they neared the end of the public comments it was evident that Tamara had more people supporting her than against. The last person to step up to the microphone was a familiar face. He introduced himself as Detective Howard Stedman with the Manitou County Sheriff's Department. He went on to say that he initially got involved when Ms. Elwell claimed some men were harassing her and trying to set her house of fire. He said, after further investigation, he believes it was just some boys that she probably urged on. He said when he talked with the homeowner it was clear Ms. Elwell and her partner were not welcome in his house, claiming he keeps nice rentals for upstanding people and he was glad to be rid of them.

"Furthermore", Stedman said, "I decided to do further investigation into Ms. Elwell's background and I found something very curious. I talked to a janitor at Blue Water State and he remembered an incident involving her. He said the scuttlebutt was that Ms. Elwell invited two male members of the track team for a ménage a trois. In case you do not know what that means, it's two men and one woman having sex".

To Find What Was Lost

Tamara jumped out of her seat and yelled, "That's a lie. That's not what happened at all."

The president told her to take a seat and she'd have her chance to talk. It took several minutes for Tamara, and for that matter the audience, to get back under control.

Detective Stedman said, "I found the school has no record of that incident but I found it curious that Ms. Elwell would give up her scholarship and quit the track team in her senior year. That's all I got to say."

Tamara was shaking so visibly that it wasn't clear that she would be able to talk. Drew left his seat and knelt in front of her. Whatever he was saying worked because she calmed down enough to get up and move to the microphone. At the same time Mr. and Mrs. Elwell were leaning over the seat trying to reach for her, but at a loss for words.

Tamara started slowly, "Everything Detective Stedman says is a lie and hearsay." The President stopped her and reminded her that this wasn't a court of law. Taking a deep breath she continued, "The two male members of the track team waited until the locker room was empty and dragged me to the equipment room. They both proceeded to rape me and left me naked and sobbing on the equipment room floor. As they were leaving I saw an assistant coach looking through the door. I thought he was there to help but he denied seeing anything and said if I filed a complaint he'd say I invited the boys in to the room. I was an emotional mess with no one to turn to and I couldn't continue on the team with the assistant coach and the two men lying about what happened. Every case that I know of involving a girl being raped by an athlete in college turns against the girl. I just wanted to complete my degree and get out of there."

Before she finished her comments Josh Erickson, still undercover, started yelling, "Down with the pervert. We don't need her teaching our kids. She's the worst kind of scum." The president was banging his gavel to no avail as the man kept yelling. Drew couldn't take it any longer and left his seat, to confront the man. Just when he got close Chief Parker wrapped his arms around him and one of his officers did the same thing to Josh. Drew watched as the loud mouth was escorted from the auditorium. The chief whispered to Drew to relax and kept saying, "Everything is okay he's one of us." Drew didn't quite understand but took the chief at his word and returned to his seat.

The president started hitting his gavel again and was finally able to regain order. When Pastor Hanson gave a signal, in unison thirty or forty people stood and start chanting, "God hates fags, Fear God not fags". The president banged his gavel again, and in a voice that couldn't be heard over the racket, one of the board members said, "I move that any decision on this matter be tabled for one week so that we can absorb the testimonies presented today, and that Tamara Elwell be suspended with pay until the board makes a final decision." There was an immediate second to the motion and with no discussion it passed unanimously.

As soon as the meeting was adjourned, Carl and Pat Elwell rushed over to Tamara and grasped her in what could best be described as a group hug. Pat kept saying "Why Tamara? Why didn't you tell us?" Tamara gave no answer but continued sobbing like a baby in her parent's arms.

To Find What Was Lost

Drew stepped in and said, "Carl and Pat, why don't you come back to my apartment and you continue talking in a quiet setting? In fact, it's a beautiful night so we can use the rooftop deck. I think it would be better than going to Tamara's place just yet. I also have an extra bedroom if you want to stay with me."

The Elwell's thanked Drew and said they would appreciate having a quiet place to talk, but they didn't need a place to stay as they had already checked into the motel located downtown. Drew suggested that Tamara ride with her parents to his apartment. She agreed but said she needed a few minutes to talk with him alone. Tamara walked to Drew's vehicle where she confronted him. "Why did you tell them about me? Don't you think I can handle things myself? I didn't want them to know about what happened at Blue Water State, and now they are going to be all over me. I don't know whether to be furious at you or thankful for you, but whatever, I'm not seeing them alone tonight. You're going to be with me."

Drew pulled her in to his arms and said, "I called everybody I could to get them out to the meeting. The chief also told me that he has an inside source who alerted him that they were going to be using some information from Blue Water State. Obviously, they don't have anything but hearsay, although sadly it's damaging. When you told me about your parents I had the sneaking suspicion that they would have your back. When I met with them at their home, and by the way I had Coney dogs with them at Angelo's, they seemed so open and honest I knew they had to be here. According to them, they did not have a major issue with your choice of a partner. Finally, you need to know that I told them I love you."

Tamara looked stunned and could barely get words out. "You told them you love me? You've never told me that and you said it to my parents. What are you doing to me? First, Kathy finds I've been unfaithful to her, and before I can figure out what I feel myself my parents arrive on the scene. Now I know for sure that you're going to suffer through this with my parents tonight, because I can't do it alone."

Drew looked at her and said, "Tamara, the elephant in the room is your love affair with the coach. You didn't bring it up tonight when you talked about being raped and never told your parents about it. It seems like you are protecting this guy and it doesn't make sense."

Tamara started crying, "Stop it, Stop it, Stop it. I couldn't tell my parents about it because I was too ashamed. I wasn't a kid I was 20 years old and fell in love with Mr. Wonderful. I was such a fool and got burned so badly. You should have seen how he looked at me after those two guys raped me. It was like I was dirt. All I could think about was getting away from it all. There was nobody there for me until I turned around and found Kathy. She didn't judge me and only wanted to do him great bodily harm. She took me in and I felt safe. She was what I thought I needed."

The Elwell's got tired of waiting and drove up next to where Tamara and Drew were standing. Drew told them he'd meet them at the apartment and left as Tamara was stepping into their car. The first question Pat Elwell asked was, "Where was Kathy tonight? We thought for sure she'd have been at the meeting."

To Find What Was Lost

Tamara had no answer and only said, "I don't know." Trying to change the subject she thanked them for coming and shared how surprised she was to see them. When they wanted to pursue the events of the evening Tamara held them off. She finally said that she wanted to wait until Drew could join them.

Pat Elwell couldn't contain herself and said, "I don't know why you haven't told us about the harassment and the fire. Did you think we would turn our backs on you? We have never done that and never would. You're our daughter and we both love you so much. All we want to do is help you through difficult times."

"It isn't you, Mom or Dad," said Tamara. "It's me. I'd done something that I'm very ashamed of and couldn't bear to share it with you. I want to handle my problems but now it looks like I really need help. Did Drew tell you he was almost killed because he was a friend of mine? He needed brain surgery and they shattered his leg all because of me. I feel like anyone I'm close to gets hurt, and it has to end." By this time both Tamara and her mother were in tears.

Tamara led them up the stairs to the second-floor apartment. She pointed down the hall and said, "That's my apartment, but we're going to Drew's because he has access to a roof deck." Both parents were complimentary about the building and how clean and fresh everything looked. They were just as surprised when they entered Drew's apartment and saw that it was totally updated. He greeted them at the bottom of the circular staircase, hopping on his good leg and told them he had a fire going in the pit. He said they arrived at the right time since he could get up and down stairs but carrying anything while doing it was a problem. The Elwell's carried up wine, glasses, crackers and cheese. One would have thought they were having a party instead of a difficult discussion.

Chapter 27

When they were all settled around the fire and each had a glass of wine Drew spoke. "Tamara, I think it's time you tell your parents everything that happened to you at Blue Water State." He reached over and took her hand in his to give her moral support.

Tamara took a few seconds to gather her thoughts and then started, "Do you remember my assistant coach on the track team? His name was Ed Conover." When both parents nodded that they remembered him she continued, "During the summer between my junior and senior year Ed accompanied me to several special training camps and then I worked with him at Blue Water State's summer sports camp for youth. During that time we became lovers. I fell totally in love with him and couldn't think of anything else except being with him."

She heard her mother gasp but continued, "Our love affair continued during the school year right through cross country and the Christmas break. We'd find places to go, away from the university, or he would take me on recruiting trips without anyone knowing. The hardest part for me to tell you is that he was married with three young children, and I thought he was going to leave his wife for me. Just before the start of the track season he told me it was over. He said that he loved his wife and would never think of leaving her. I was just a student in love with her older coach and that I got what I wanted out of it too. I tried all sorts of ways to contact him but he shut me off. One day I whispered that I was going to tell his wife and he went ballistic."

"It was less than a week later when the two men from the track team pulled me into the empty equipment room and raped me. I saw Ed standing at the door and yelled for him to help but he turned and walked away. When I got myself together and put clothes on I found him in his office. His look was so cold that just thinking of it sends shivers down my spine. He said if I told anyone what happened between us he was prepared to say that he saw me invite those two boys into the equipment room. He kept going on about what would happen to my reputation and I panicked. Maybe it was an anxiety attack or shock but I really don't remember the next couple of days."

"When I started to come back to reality I was in my dorm room and Kathy was sitting by my side. We had been friendly but not close friends. She was a runner and we often jogged together during the off season. Apparently she found me wandering outside the gym and recognized that something was wrong. She kept me calm, and I felt safe in her presence. Together we decided that I would quit the team and move into her apartment for the remainder of the year. She helped me get a job to cover expenses and was my savior at that time. We didn't become lovers till we met up again much later when she was a rep for a running shoe company and I was competing in open races but I'll never forget how she cared for me at Blue Water. I know you're wondering why didn't I come to you for help. All I can say is that I was feeling so full of shame and embarrassment I couldn't face you. You would have been so disappointed in me and rightfully so."

Without talking beforehand, the Elwell's and Drew seemed to be on the same page. They both questioned her decision not to go to the police. They both thought the boys should have been charged with rape and that she should have filed a complaint with the school about the coach's behavior. No matter how many ways they put it Tamara couldn't see their point. She was convinced that athletes are never found guilty and she would be the one ridiculed in public.

When Carl Elwell suggested that Kathy may have taken advantage of her during a moment of emotional distress Tamara didn't go into a rage but kept saying, "That's not how it was".

Drew knew he was on dangerous ground if he continued to pursue this point with Tamara. He quickly realized that to say Kathy took advantage of her during a weak moment would only force Tamara to defend the relationship. She already felt guilty for the events leading up to quitting the team, and this would only make her feel bad to think Kathy took advantage. So, he took control of the conversation and said that it had been a difficult night on everyone, especially Tamara. He said, "Let's only talk about more positive things. I'm sure you want to catch up on the rest of the family and everything at home."

Drew excused himself and went downstairs to give the Elwell's some privacy. In about half an hour they all came down to Drew's apartment and said their goodbyes. Drew heard them make plans to have breakfast together, and overall their spirits seemed good considering the circumstances.

After they left Tamara faced Drew and said, "I really can't go back to my apartment tonight. Would you mind if I spend the night? I'm meeting my parents for breakfast at nine, and by that time Kathy will be out of the apartment. I'm just not ready to deal with her yet."

Drew didn't know what to expect, but he got his answer soon enough when Tamara went into his bedroom. She got a tee shirt out of his dresser as if she had done it a dozen times, and then went into the bathroom and closed the door. Drew hollered to her that there was a new toothbrush in the bottom drawer down in the vanity, but he didn't hear a reply. When he heard the shower turn on he figured he might as well go to bed. He must have been tired, because as soon as his head hit the pillow he was asleep. It wasn't until he felt his bed move that he remembered Tamara was with him. She reached over to kiss his cheek and he felt her damp hair on his neck.

Drew turned over and took her in his arms. They laid without talking for a while, and then Tamara told him how thankful she was to have him in her corner. There was no other talking, but both of them were awake for a couple of hours before sleep took over.

When Drew woke up the other side of the bed was empty. The newness of their relationship made him anxious, especially when he saw something such as an empty bed. Even when he knew his mind was playing tricks on him it didn't stop him from thinking she had to get away from him or that she'd second doubts and run back to Kathy. Everything about his relationship with Tamara was new ground for him, but he wouldn't change a thing. When he walked into the kitchen he found Tamara wearing his tee shirt over her undies, standing in front of the window drinking coffee. Seeing Drew she smiled and said, "Thanks for last night. I really needed that."

Tamara went back to her apartment to get dressed so she could meet her parents for breakfast. Drew had physical therapy at 10:00, but it was very clear that neither of them wanted to part. Drew suddenly had an idea and said, "How about after your parents head home you come with me to Traverse City? I'm looking at some new awnings for the three shops, and I'd love your company and opinion as well. Besides, if you stay here all you'll be thinking of is how you should be in school."

Tamara really didn't have to think about it. As soon as he made the offer she was ready to go. They agreed to leave as soon as he got back from therapy and would grab lunch in one of the many great eating places in Traverse. As Tamara was walking down the corridor, Jimmy Hanson came up the stairs. She still wasn't feeling easy around him but managed to greet him with a simple hello. Jimmy smiled and acknowledged her before asking if she knew where Drew was? She told him he had left for physical therapy and really wouldn't be back the rest of the day.

It was then on a whim that Tamara asked, "Jimmy, you've promised that you've been no part of the harassment and assaults on me and I believe you. What I'm wondering is if you have any way to get me into your father's church. I mean I want to go there at night and look around his office. With the meeting coming up next week I want to find anything I can to protect myself. I'd really appreciate it."

Jimmy looked doubtful but then said, "I can get you in but if we were ever caught we'd be in deep doo doo. We'd have to go after midnight to be sure no one else was around. I think the best time would be Thursday or Friday this week. I'll do anything to help Drew and you to see that I am not involved. Drew has been a really good friend to me, and between the construction job and the extra work Drew gives me here, I finally have my head above water. The best part is Drew is helping me save. He put together a plan where I won't buy anything until I have the money to pay cash. I'm saving nearly 30% of my paycheck. He's a really good businessman and he's even helping me in my job so that I'll be more valuable to Mike Edwards."

As far as the plans to visit the church went, Tamara's Willy's Jeepster's so identifiable they agreed to use Jimmy's pick-up. He told her to meet him at 12:00 midnight on Thursday in the parking area behind the apartments. Tamara had no idea what she was looking for, but doing nothing wasn't helping either, so she figured nothing ventured, nothing gained.

The trip to Traverse City with Drew was a pleasant break for her. On the way there she talked about breakfast with her parents and, they talked about northern Michigan while enjoying the scenery. They kept the conversation away from the school hearing although sometimes that was difficult when it was such an important issue. Tamara didn't mention her plans to investigate the church after hours, nor was she ever planning to tell Drew. They decided to have lunch before looking at awnings. Drew told her that he saw in the Traverse City Record Eagle that Chef Mario Batali named two places in Traverse as his favorite spots to eat.

The one they chose to eat at was a sandwich shop called Frenchies. The restaurant was in a tiny building that looked like it might fall down during a strong wind, but it had lots of charm. There were only a couple of tables inside, but outside there were more tables. The waitress led them along a narrow sidewalk to the rear of the building where there were four more tables. The lunch crowd was leaving so there were tables available. They both picked the pastrami sandwich and weren't disappointed.

The awning shop was located on the outskirts of Traverse City towards Acme. Drew had a copy of the historic commission's guidelines about awnings. They were very specific and basically wanted the awnings to look similar to those used in the 1890's. It didn't take Drew long to identify a couple of awnings that he thought would look good in front of the three retail spaces. Tamara picked the one she liked and Drew went with that selection.

Tamara didn't have a clue about Drew's financial situation. She knew that he sold a couple of car washes a year ago but couldn't imagine they provided enough money for him to live on for a year plus buy the business block downtown. On the way back he talked about some ideas he was considering regarding a couple of other properties in Manitou. It was clear to her that Drew was planting some roots in town and wouldn't be leaving any time soon.

When they arrived back in Manitou it was dinner time, and Tamara told Drew she had to find Kathy. Drew tried to get her to share her feelings but Tamara only said she had to resolve some issues. When she got back to her apartment

Kathy was in the kitchen heating up some leftover chili. The silence was intolerable, and finally Tamara spoke.

"Kathy, I can understand that you're hurt and threatened because I've developed a relationship with Drew. I won't deny that I have feelings for him, and we have a sexual relationship too. But, on the other hand you never showed up the night of the school board hearing. I needed support and you weren't there. Do you know who was there? My parents. Yes, they were there to lend me support. Do you know why they were there? Drew drove to Flint and met with them because he knew how much I needed people to support me. In case you're interested, the board decided to suspend me with pay, but that didn't hurt half as much as you not being there for me."

Laying down the ladle Kathy looked at Tamara. "I'm glad you had people to support you because I was so pissed at you I'd have been no help. I rescued you at Blue Water State and you return the favor by falling for a man who helps you out of one difficult spot. I was the one you could rely on and you gave that up to be comforted by Drew. How can you possibly think that I'd have been at the hearing? You hurt me, and there was no way I could make you feel better at that time. I wanted you to hurt like I hurt."

Tamara was stunned by Kathy's statement. "You don't wish pain on someone you truly love. What you're saying doesn't make sense. You're telling me that you are mad because Drew was there to help when I needed it. On top of that my parents were shocked that I thought they were opposed to our relationship. They said they only wanted me to be happy and didn't understand what happened at Blue Water State.

To Find What Was Lost

You were the one who convinced me not to talk to my
parents about the love affair or the rape. You convinced me
that they were having a hard time with our relationship. For
the past three years I have avoided them, not knowing that I
was really hurting them. All they want to do is love me."

"That's all I want to do to Tam"

"No Kathy, you want to control me and convince me that
you're the only one who really loves me. At the same time
it's cool for you to go away and hook up with other women.
You just don't get it. I don't know where we go from here but
I can tell you I don't see my future with you. I'm going to
move into the second bedroom until I decide what to do."

Strangely enough there weren't many tears shed during the
conversation. Maybe they both knew that their relationship
was changing and the tears had already been shed. Tamara
went into the bedroom and moved her personal belongings
to the second bedroom. Meanwhile, after Kathy finished
eating the reheated chili, she called to Tamara that there was
still some chili left if she wanted it.

In a few minutes Tamara came out of the bedroom and got a
bowl of chili. Kathy poured her a glass of wine and they sat
together at the table. Kathy asked her to tell her about the
hearing. She was surprised that the detective had been able
to find out about the incidents at Blue Water State and
wasn't surprised that she was suspended with pay. When she
asked Tamara what was going to happen next, Tamara
stunned her.

"Tonight, at midnight I'm meeting Jimmy Hanson, and he's going to get me into the office of the Living Spirit Evangelical Church. I don't know what I'll find, but I'm searching for anything that will help me. I'm convinced that Hanson is behind everything that has happened to me and maybe, just maybe, I'll find an answer there."

"Please let me go with you," pleaded Kathy. "I don't want you going there alone with Jimmy. Give me a chance to make it up to you. If not that, let me at least support you tonight. I'm not going to take no for an answer. I assume you haven't told Drew about this, and if you don't let me go, I'll tell him."

All Tamara could think was that Kathy was giving mixed signals again. For the first time she saw Kathy as a user and wondered if she took advantage of her when she imploded at State. Both her parents and Drew touched on that last night and she refused to hear it. On the other hand, she really liked the idea of Kathy going with them and knew it'd make her more comfortable.

At midnight both Tamara and Kathy, doing their best to imitate cat burglars, were dressed in all black and waiting behind the apartments in the parking area. Jimmy's beat-up pickup drove to where they were standing and they both hopped in. Tamara explained to Jimmy that Kathy wanted to come and she wanted her with her. Jimmy didn't put up any fuss about it and said that he expected the place to be deserted and they should be able to get in and out of there without a problem.

They parked in the same two track dirt road where Jimmy had parked before then followed him through the woods and across the field to the church. He gave a hip check and a pull up to the door of the maintenance room and it opened the same as always. Using flashlights, the three walked through the building and went immediately to the church office. It took a while to get into the pastor's office until Jimmy found a key in the top drawer of the secretary's desk. They started exploring the office, and Tamara went immediately to the desk where she searched each drawer. They only thing of interest she found was a note from Detective Stedman about the suspected trouble Tamara had at Blue Water State. As far as she could see they didn't have any more information and didn't have the names of the assistant coach or the two male students who raped her.

Kathy was going through the file cabinets when all of a sudden she said, "Holy shit! You won't believe what I've found. Tamara and Jimmy rushed to Kathy as she pulled half a dozen file folders from the file cabinets. She set them on the desk so all could see, and then proceeded to talk.

"I have six folders here that show these people have signed their home and savings over to the church. At first I didn't pay any attention till I saw that one of the names was my grandpa. I did a quick scan of the material in his folder and it appears that the church promises they will take care of him for life if he signs everything over to them now. The way it's written I don't think there's any guarantee that he'll be cared for the rest of his life. This is really a shock to me because I didn't know he was even involved with this church."

They skimmed over the next five files and saw the same thing. People were signing over everything to the church, with the promise that the church would take care of them.

Tamara asked Jimmy where the copy machine was and followed him to the secretary's office. They turned the machine on and waited what seemed like hours for it to warm up. Finally they were able to copy the essential pages of each file.

As they were putting the folder back in the file cabinet they heard cars pulling into the gravel lot outside and all three looked at each other with fear in their eyes. Jimmy immediately took over and first asked if they had their cell phones. Both of them answered in the affirmative. Then he told them to go back through the maintenance room and get out of the building as fast as they could. He said that he would make up some story about hunting for money because he had lost some at the casino. He joked that it was something that he had done in the past so his father would most likely believe him.

Tamara and Kathy made it to the maintenance room just as they heard people entering the church. Tamara couldn't help herself and opened the door a crack to see Pastor Hanson and Detective Stedman rushing to the office. They heard Jimmy holler, "Hey, it's just me." They could only imagine the story he was going to tell them. They hurried through the woods and knew they better stay away from where Jimmy had parked his truck. Kathy, having lived in Manitou her whole life, knew that if they walked another quarter of a mile through the field they would come out on a totally different road from the church.

Tamara dreaded making the phone call but didn't feel there was any other option. Kathy said, "Tell him we'll be on the corner of Field Drive and Verona Avenue. That's all he needs to know. In the mean time we'll just stay in the wooded area."

Drew received the call about 1:30 am and questioned in his mind whether middle of the night calls were commonplace in Michigan. As soon as he heard Tamara's voice his heart started racing. She remained remarkably calm on the other side of the line and simply said that she needed to be picked up on the corner of Field Drive and Verona. One would have thought she was calling for a taxi. When Drew asked for further explanation, she told him to get there quickly and she'd fill him in. When she finished the call, Kathy hugged her and said everything would be all right. But for the first time in years, Kathy's hug felt more like a gesture from a friend.

They saw Drew's car turn the corner and ran out into the street to greet it. He parked and got out just as they arrived at the door. Tamara threw her arms around him and said she was never so glad to see someone. Drew looked her in the eyes and then Tamara leaned in close and kissed him on the lips. All the while Kathy was watching this display and looked away in resignation.

When they got back to Drew's apartment Tamara laid the copies they had made at the church on the table. What we have here is evidence that he is scamming old people into signing over their homes and savings. We have six people here, but who knows how many others he has scammed. Drew briefly looked at them and said that it was certainly something they should bring to the chief's attention. Tamara also told him that Detective Stedman was with the pastor when they got to the church. Drew was upset that they had involved Jimmy in their espionage and said he would check on him first thing in the morning.

It was now after 2:00 a.m., and Drew suggested they call it a night. It was at that point that he fully realized his relationship with Tamara had turned a corner. Tamara turned to Kathy, gave her a hug and said, "I'll see you in the morning." Without waiting for any acknowledgement from Kathy or Drew she turned and walked into his bedroom. Kathy, looking terribly sad, hugged Drew and said, "You know I love her. Please take care of her."

When Drew got in the bedroom Tamara said it quick and simple. "I realized tonight that I ran to Kathy in a time of need. Although I didn't doubt my love at that time, it was clear to me that she recognized my weakened state and used it to her advantage. Now I find myself in a similar situation. Two times I have run to you, but I want you to know I won't be taken advantage of again."

"When I look at you I see a strong woman, a woman who feels things deeply, a woman who gives her love sincerely. I'll never take advantage of you because the qualities that make you vulnerable are also the qualities that make you a person with depth of character. I told you a few weeks ago that there was something going on between us and that I'd never give up trying to win you over. I still feel that way. Each and every day I'll work to win your heart, even when you've already given it to me."

Chapter 28

Shortly after waking up, Tamara started talking to Drew about the information she found at the church. "It's very clear to me that the church is getting old people to sign over their homes and life savings. This pastor must be a piece of work to take advantage of older people like that. For the first time I realize his views about same sex relationships aren't as important as his actions toward helpless senior citizens. He was just using same sex relationships to hook in frightened older people."

Drew looked at her, and while he agreed with her point about the pastor, he also had seen enough detective shows to know that law enforcement would have trouble acting on information obtained illegally. He thought that their best chance to expose Pastor Hanson's plot with senior citizens was to get Kathy's grandfather to testify. He didn't have the slightest idea if Kathy's grandfather would do it, but no matter what, they had to get Kathy onboard.

Drew spoke, "I think you need to get Kathy onboard with us. She'd have the most influence over her grandfather. Since it's one of her relatives who's involved, she may get over any hurt feelings she has about losing you. If you can talk to her, the three of us can go to the chief and plead our case."

Tamara didn't argue, in fact, she agreed with Drew and said, "Kathy loves her grandfather and I know it is killing her to think that someone is taking advantage of him. I'll get with her first thing this morning and hopefully we can meet with the Chief before noon."

Tamara was surprised that Kathy was as open to meeting with her as she was. At the same time Kathy seemed resigned to the fact that their relationship was over, but her feelings for Tamara wouldn't allow her to walk away from the situation. Because of Tamara's urging, Kathy agreed to meet with the Police chief and do everything she could to convince him to investigate the case involving her grandfather.

Drew didn't know if it was the chief's relationship with his mother that made things go so easily or if the chief was really concerned. All he had to do was make one call, and the chief set up a meeting for eleven o'clock in his office. Never in his life had a public official responded so quickly to any request he made. Tamara, Kathy and Drew arrived at the police station a little before 11:00 a.m. and were immediately directed into the Chief Parker's office. They were surprised to see two other people in the office. One of the people was a man who looked familiar to Drew and Tamara. They both seemed to remember why he looked familiar at the same time and looked at each other in surprise.

The chief stood up and said, "Let me introduce you to Josh Erickson, on loan to our department by the Michigan State Police, and Stephanie Willis, an agent with the Federal Bureau of Investigation. You might have remembered Josh from the school board hearing, but what you didn't know he is on our side."

"Our original idea was to keep Officer Erickson away from the Manitou Police Station but that changed when Agent Willis contacted me yesterday. It seems our good pastor has a history of convincing older folks to turn over their assets to him. Drew led me to believe you had some information regarding older members of our community and I thought it was best to involve Erickson and Willis in our meeting."

Tamara and Kathy shared their adventure of the previous evening. They didn't tell them anything about Jimmy Hanson and made it appear as if they found these files. They laid out the photocopies of the information they took from the file. It clearly showed that six families had given everything to the church. Kathy talked at length about her grandfather and how lonely he had been since her grandmother's death. She noted that recently he seemed to be talking more about religion than she ever remembered before. She had talked to her parents about it and they blew it off as age-related. She explained that it looks as if Pastor Hanson promised him perpetual care until he dies, but she couldn't find any evidence they were prepared to provide that.

FBI Agent Willis spoke up at this point and said, "Pastor Hanson has successfully pulled off scams like this in both Indianapolis and Fort Wayne. I was surprised when I heard he was in a little northern Michigan city because it didn't seem like his typical location, but after looking at the demographics of the county, everything fits. You have a very high percentage of low to medium income, white senior citizens. He is an expert at preying on their fears. In Indianapolis and Fort Wayne, he focused on the government taking control of their lives including their weapons. In Manitou, the fears he hit on were social change, same sex marriage and homosexuality."

"That's right," said Josh Erickson. "I 've managed to get into a few of the council meetings. They don't fully trust me yet, but they are getting there. I also have hung around with some of the council members after hours. Pastor Hanson personally told me that he targeted Tamara because she has no support here. He said that Kathy's parents are well established in the community, and if anything happened to her, people would react. With Tamara she is an outsider and deserves what's coming to her. I'm also sorry to say that the Muellers, Kathy's parents, have attended the church on occasion, and they gave Pastor Hanson the impression that Kathy's life would be better if Tamara wasn't in it. You also have to keep in mind that Detective Stedman is a major player in the church and there was no way he was going to solve any crimes perpetrated against you."

Chief Parker told them that the information they obtained by some unknown means couldn't be used in court. They could use the names of the people who have turned everything over to the church and start talking to them and their relatives. He went on to say that the case was turning in the direction of fraud. He added, "Hanson preys on the fears of people to attract them to his church and then finds the weakest among them. He is very clever at building a council consisting of some pretty angry men. These are men who would do anything to stop their worst fears from coming true. In your case, Tamara and Kathy, the fear he used to polarize his members was same sex relationships, and indeed you were at risk for serious injury, up to and including death."

Throughout the meeting FBI Agent Willis couldn't keep her eyes off of Kathy. Whenever she spoke she looked at Kathy, to the exclusion of the others. There were a couple of times when she made a gesture and her hand landed conveniently on Kathy's arm. Although Tamara wasn't all that familiar with the lesbian culture, she knew when someone was hitting on another person, and Kathy was being hit on.

The plan was that Agent Willis would investigate the families, particularly working with Kathy to get her grandfather to step forward. Meanwhile, undercover officer Erickson would try to find out what was going on in the inner circle. There was nothing for Tamara and Drew to do and that left them feeling helpless. After the meeting, Tamara, Kathy and Drew were standing outside the Police Department and saw Detective Stedman entering the building. Out of frustration Tamara hollered, "Detective, have you arrested anyone for setting fire to our house yet?"

"Looks just like I told you, kid's pulling a prank that went south. I've closed the case. If you have a complaint talk to the sheriff." With that he opened the door and walked in. As he was standing at the reception desk he saw Josh Erickson talking comfortably with Chief Parker. Josh didn't see him and Stedman turned and walked out of the building immediately without being seen.

Kathy looked at Tamara and said, "I had no idea my parents ever attended that church. You have to believe me." She stopped suddenly and said she had to get back to the shop. As she was turning to leave her phone rang. She talked for a minute and it was obvious she was setting up a meeting time. When she ended the call she looked at Tamara and said, "That's different. Stephanie Willis had some more questions to ask me so we're meeting after I close the shop."

"Did she want me there too?"

"No, she just wanted to see me. I imagine it's about my grandfather." And with that Kathy walked to her car so quickly that she didn't hear Tamara say, "I bet."

That left Drew and Tamara standing alone in front of the police station. Drew wanted to say something such as *That went well,* but good judgment took over and he kept quiet. By not commenting, it allowed Tamara to express her feelings.

"I could say my life is breaking apart. I'm targeted by some "holier than thou" religious group, my car is keyed, my house set on fire, we're physically attacked, I'm harassed on the job, publicly humiliated, and I break up with my lover. I should be in a mental hospital but I'm not, and I have you to thank for that. In the middle of this mess I found you, and for some crazy reason I feel okay right now. That explanation does sound kind of nuts, doesn't it?"

Drew responded, "The only part I care about is that we found each other. I was lost, and for me, finding you gave me something to live for. For the past two years I hadn't been living, just getting by. I can't predict our future together, but because of you I know I'm going to be okay no matter what lies ahead."

Tamara had something on her mind, but she didn't want to share her idea with Drew. She'd need a different car since hers is so identifiable. She asked Drew if he needed his rental car this afternoon because her car wasn't running right and she had to run some errands. She feared that Drew would want to accompany her, but he simply said that she could take it. He later added that he had to do some exercises his

physical therapist gave him and then he was going to get off
his leg.

Chapter 29

Howard Stedman couldn't wait to get to the church to meet with the pastor. He smelled something funny with that new guy and to see him with the chief and those lesbos just leaving the police station answered his question. He had to file a couple of investigative reports back at the Manitou Sheriff's Department and that would give him time to grab a bite to eat before the meeting.

Stedman had warned Hanson that he was pushing the lesbian thing too hard and that he could overdo it and ruin everything. He first met Pastor Hanson a couple of years ago when a family complained that the good Pastor was stealing their elderly mother's money. Initially he didn't put much stock in it, but with very little effort he learned that the old man had cashed in over $40,000 in savings bonds in order to give the money to the pastor. It didn't take much effort to figure out the little pipsqueak of a pastor was raking in big dough.

Stedman had more than enough to charge Pastor Hanson with theft and fraud but he had bigger and better ideas. He had Pastor Hanson in a no win situation and offered himself as the solution. However, the solution was going to cost Hanson 50% of the take. What he would offer the Pastor in return was a complete investigation on every candidate the Pastor wanted to hit up for money. Stedman would check into the background of the mark and determine whether they were a good target. He'd find out if they had any family left to care about them and also where their money was kept.

To Find What Was Lost

His plan was working very well, and in a little more than two years they had amassed over $800,000.00. They formed a dummy corporation called Christians Serving Christians and transferred the money there first. From there it went to a children's charity in Aruba which of course was the dummy corporation. The long-range plan was for Stedman and Hanson to set up accounts in Aruba which would make it easy to transfer funds from the children's charity to their personal account. Stedman checked the phony charity regularly and knew the pastor hadn't taken anything out of it yet.

They did spend a little money making up phony brochures, letterhead and setting up the dummy corporations. What they created looked so real the elderly victims actually thought their money was safe and protected. The Pastor was lucky that Stedman joined him when he did. Stedman quickly identified 6 people that were risky candidates, and the pastor backed off. He had to give it to the pastor. The man really knew how to get people opening their pocketbooks while they all thought he was opening the gates of heaven for them.

It did seem strange to him that people so willing to hate gays, blacks or immigrants thought they'd be welcomed by Jesus - the same Jesus who was dark skinned and loved the poor, downtrodden and sinners. Stedman often chuckled when he thought about their crazy religion and was glad his Jewish roots gave him a different set of values. It also amazed him that there was so much money in a small town, and one would never guess the wealth of some senior citizens. Most of the people they scammed were fearful of the government, drove older automobiles and lived in unpretentious homes. The last thing they wanted was to attract anyone's attention to them or their financial savings.

Stedman introduced some new ideas into their scam. One thing he did was to identify wealthy elderly people who had no church. It was simple to knock on their doors and introduce himself as being with the Manitou Sheriff's Department. His next step was to introduce Pastor Hanson as a person who volunteered his time with the sheriff's department to check in on seniors and see if they had any special needs.

Once the introduction was made the pastor did his thing. He helped these elderly people with advice about bad deals, ran errands for them, hooked them up with Meals on Wheels and visited at least once a week. He never tried to get them to attend church. In fact, his real goal was to keep their names off of any church record. Very few people knew the pastor was even visiting them. When the hook was firmly set, he talked to them about his perpetual care program. For someone in the later stages of life and without any family, the pastor's plan to take care of them till the end sounded pretty good. At this very moment, there were three more people ready to sign over their estate to the pastor, and the estates were each worth more than $200,000.

There was one other deed that Stedman performed that even the pastor was unaware of. Two of the oldest targets on their list, both in their early 90's, suffered from congestive heart failure. Stedman helped them along the way to a great afterlife with an overdose of digitalis. The medical examiner observed them, established a time of death and sent the bodies on to the funeral home. In each case there was no family remaining, and everyone just assumed their time had come.

Chapter 30

When Stedman left the sheriff's office about 5:30 pm, he didn't notice the car parked on the side street. Tamara started the car as soon as she saw Stedman and followed close enough to see his tail lights. When he pulled into the church parking lot, Tamara drove on by. She circled around and drove down the now familiar two track where Jimmy had parked the other night. Leaving the car there she ran through the woods and across the field to the back side of the church.

The door to the maintenance room opened when she mimicked Jimmy's action of the other night. She could hear voices talking and had to get closer to the office to understand them. Getting into the main body of the church was no easy task. First, the door leading into the hallway squeaked like fingernails on a chalkboard. Without knowing if there were men outside, it required her to duck walk across the sanctuary, being careful not to raise her head above the chairs.

Once clear of the sanctuary she was able to enter the corridor leading to the office. She could hear Stedman talking to someone and quickly realized it was Pastor Hanson. Stedman used his Christian name when addressing him. "Now listen to me Ralph, I know what I saw, and it was evident to me that fellow Jack Thompson was real friendly with Chief Parker. On top of that, Mueller and Elwell had just walked out of the station when I arrived. Give me a few minutes with Thompson and I'll get the truth."

"Howie don't get so excited. They don't have anything on us. They're so focused on protecting the gays and lesbians from discrimination that they have totally missed what we're really doing. You may be right about Thompson but he hasn't seen or heard anything that doesn't make him believe we are anything more than a bunch of backwoods bigots."

Tamara was stretched out on the floor trying to hear everything being said when suddenly she heard the entry door open. She quietly scrambled down the corridor beyond the office where the light from the office partially lit the corridor. She clearly saw Josh Erickson, the undercover officer, enter the office. As soon as he was in the office she hurried back to her previous position. Both Pastor Hanson and Detective Stedman turned in surprise as the man they had just been talking about entered the office.

Pastor Hanson spoke first. "I wasn't expecting to see you tonight Jack. What's on your mind?"

"Well, Rev, I was just worried that that teacher was going to get off without being punished. I heard rumors that she may not even lose her job. I wanted to know if you needed me to do anything about it. I'm with you. Just tell me what to do."

Stedman jumped in, "Strange you should say you're with us. I just happened to be at the police department today and saw you there. Mind telling us what you were up to?" Stedman intentionally left out the part about seeing Erickson with Chief Parker and that other woman, or that Mueller and Elwell just left the station.

"I was just there filing a complaint because my car had been broken into." I wanted to get the complaint number for my insurance company. Why do you ask"?

Stedman smelled blood. Thompson, or whatever his name is was lying and he was ready to catch him in it. "So tell me Thompson, do people usually report a break-in directly to the chief with the two lesbos and their favorite boy toy looking on"

Erickson tried to tough it out and said, "This is bull shit I don't need to have you accuse me of this crap."

As he turned to leave Detective Stedman said, "I have a gun on you right now so don't take another step. Now turn around and slowly empty your pockets on the table."

Not thinking this would be a real undercover job Erickson had left his Michigan State Police badge pinned to his wallet. It was so shiny and bright there was no way he could conceal it. Detective Stedman took out his handcuffs and cuffed Erickson before he frisked him. He quickly found and removed the IWB holster with a 40 S & W tucked inside. He wasn't carrying any other weapon. Going through his wallet he found identification for Josh Erickson.

Before Erickson knew what hit him Stedman punched him full force in the face. The nose broke immediately, and blood started running down his face. He pushed him into a chair and calmly said, "Now Mr. Thompson, or is it Erickson? I want you to tell me why you were with the police chief." When Erickson didn't speak Stedman punched him again. From that point on Erickson was a punching bag and Stedman seemed to revel with each strike. Erickson cried out with each punch but still wouldn't say anything.

To Find What Was Lost

Tamara couldn't take it any longer. This man was being beaten because of her. She grabbed her cell phone, but in the darkened hallway, didn't have time to fuss with finding 911. She hadn't added Drew to her speed dial list so she hit "1" on her speed dial which was Kathy's phone. When Kathy answered, Tamara heard lots of background noise. Then she remembered Kathy was meeting up with the FBI Agent. She whispered as quietly as possible, "Kathy, help me, I'm at Hanson's church and they are going to kill that undercover guy."

Kathy put her hand over her ear to block out noise and said, "What?"

Tamara then heard Pastor Hanson yell, "Stop, stop you're going to kill him."

Stedman was quiet for a moment and then said, "The trouble with you Ralph is you don't like to see the dirty work done. You wouldn't have complained if that Elwell girl burned up in her house. You probably aren't opposed to me getting rid of this piece of shit as long as your hands aren't dirty. I think that sometimes you get confused and think you're a regular preacher instead of a con artist and crook."

"Look Howie, we've done really well but now's the time to end it. If this guy really is a cop and infiltrated our group, then the question is who sent him? We each have almost a half a million. Let's not be greedy and push it."

"That's where you're wrong Ralph. I'm going to have almost a million. No need to worry about you." With that statement, he picked up Erickson's gun and shot pastor one time through the head.

Josh Erickson was lying on the floor and couldn't believe his eyes. He yelled, "Stedman, put the gun down!"

Stedman had a sneer on his face when he said, "Oh, I'm going to put your gun down all right because it has served its purpose." He reached down to his ankle holster and withdrew his throwaway gun, a Glock 9mm. Pushing Erickson onto his back he fired directly into his chest. Erickson took a couple of quick breaths and expired.

Tamara panicked at the sound of the gunfire and ran to get out of the building the same way she came in. Stedman heard the noise in the building but by the time he got to the sanctuary no one was there. He then heard an outside door slam on the side of the building where the furnace and maintenance room was located. He raced into the room and saw the outside door open. When he got to the door he saw a woman sprinting across the field and entering the woods. He took a shot at her but knew at that range the Glock was just about useless.

He turned and re-entered the building thinking, *that dumb queer hasn't gotten away from me.* His immediate thoughts were on setting up the scene in the pastor's office. The first thing he did was to take off the handcuffs and sit Erickson up. He took his throwaway gun and put it in Pastor Hanson's hand while squeezing the trigger to fire another shot at Erickson. Then he took Erickson's gun put it in his hand and squeezed the trigger so that both the pastor and Erickson would have blowback from the guns being shot.

Stedman took some time arranging the bodies so that it looked like they shot each other. He knew forensics in this day and age would eventually figure out where the victims were at the time of the shooting, but he was hoping by that time he would be long gone. He had one last detail to take care of and that was ridding the world of Tamara Elwell.

Tamara knew if she could get to the door she could outrun Stedman. Once she hit the field she sprinted as if she was finishing the 800 meter event at State. She didn't look back and wasn't sure Stedman had even seen her till a shot rang out. In the woods her pace slowed down, so that by the time she reached the car she was breathing naturally, and her pulse had probably returned to her training rate of 128. She reached for her phone but it was missing. Somewhere on the run she must have dropped it.

In a panic and not thinking clearly, she drove to the apartments and ran up the stairs. First, she banged on Drew's door. There was no answer. Then she went to her apartment. It was empty. Grabbing the phone she dialed 911 and told the operator there had been a shooting at the Living Spirit Evangelical Church. The 911 operator kept her on the line to get the necessary information. All the while Tamara was listening to hear if Stedman had followed her. As soon as she hung up from 911 she called Kathy. This time she could speak in her regular voice and was able to communicate with her. Kathy's first response was, "Where the heck are you? I couldn't understand anything from that last call."
"There's been a shooting at Hanson's Church, and I think both Pastor Hanson and that undercover officer are dead. I was hiding outside and I saw Stedman go into the office. He

heard me running from the building and fired a shot at me when I ran across the field."

"What? Wait. What? I'm confused. Where are you now?"

'I'm in the apartment throwing some things in a bag and getting out of here. I have to get away. He's coming for me." She must have slammed the phone down because that was all Kathy heard. She turned to Stephanie Willis, the FBI Agent, and Drew, who was also sitting at the table and said, "We've got to get to my apartment. Tamara said there's been a shooting at the church and Stedman is chasing her. She sounds really distraught and was talking about packing a bag and running."

The three jumped from their chairs and Agent Willis was on her phone calling Chief Parker as they ran from the pub. Someone at the reception desk answered the phone. Willis identified herself and then told them to listen very carefully. She reported everything that Kathy had told her and then had to get their attention so that she could give the police the right address. As she finished, the officer told her that the chief was already answering a 911 call about a shooting at the church.

Tamara was having a panic attack for sure and making all the wrong decisions. Her only thought was to flee, and yet she knew she needed to pack some clothes and things to do that. She grabbed a travel bag and rushed about the bedroom throwing in clothes and cosmetics. Zipping the bag shut she hurried from the apartment and was almost to the stairs when she saw Stedman near the top. Stedman raised his gun and aimed it at Tamara. He was prepared to shoot when Drew hollered, "Stedman stop!"

Stedman turned and looked down at Drew hobbling up the stairs. He aimed his gun at Drew when Tamara, forgetting all her fears, literally flew several feet through the air, hitting Stedman's back about shoulder high where he was standing on the stairs. Holding him tightly they both somersaulted down the stairs, landing at the feet of Agent Willis. Both Drew and Kathy rushed to Tamara who seemed to have survive the fall without any major injuries. The same couldn't be said for Stedman as he was unconscious.

To be on the safe side Agent Willis collected his fire arm and frisked him for any other weapons. She did notice the empty ankle holster and searched the stairway but couldn't find another weapon. As she was putting on the handcuffs she noticed his wrist was twisted in a funny angle, so she thought it would be better not to cuff him. Stedman started to regain consciousness and immediately complained about his wrist. Then when he saw Tamara he attempted to play the cop role and accuse her of killing Pastor Hanson. He tried to tell them that when he entered the church he saw her running from it. He found both Pastor Hanson and some other guy dead. Stedman pleaded with the FBI Agent to arrest her, but Stephanie held her ground and told him he was under arrest.

When the first police officer arrived on the scene Agent Willis informed him that Detective Stedman was under arrest and was to be put in jail after being treated at the hospital. The officer called in the information and realized there was nothing else to do at the apartment building other than wait for another officer so they could accompany Stedman to the hospital.

Getting Stedman settled in the ambulance allowed Willis to focus her attention on Tamara. Both Kathy and Drew were hovering over her, and that reminded her of two Big Horn rams butting heads to earn the right to mate with the top female. Her fantasy ended quickly as Kathy left Tamara's side and gave Stephanie a hug. Kathy said, "Thanks for taking care of that goon. I never liked him even when I was a teenager. He loved going to the favorite make out spots for the teens and harassing them. A couple of times he made some kids who were only partially clothed stand outside their car and wait there until their parents picked them up. He's a piece of work, and you were something else the way you handled him."

Stephanie seemed embarrassed by Kathy's comments and said, "Tamara is the real hero. He had Drew dead to rights and if she hadn't tackled him, Drew would be dead now."

"Yeah," Kathy said in a snarly voice, "She was something else too. Goes to show what you'll do for love." Drew and Tamara both heard her statement, but neither responded.

Chapter 31

Stephanie's phone rang, and when she finished the call she told the others that the chief would he here in less than a half an hour. Drew invited them up to his apartment where he'd get them something to drink while they waited. They all walked up so quietly one would think they were going to church. Once seated Drew got drinks for all of them. Tamara and Stephanie both chose soft drinks since they were going to be doing most of the talking once the Chief arrived. Kathy and Drew each had a beer. Tamara was starting to say something, but Stephanie said that it was best for her to wait for the chief before she talked.

"Okay, I understand that, but can I ask where you were? I tried calling from the church but couldn't speak loud enough."

"Remember, I told you that Steph, aah, Agent Willis was continuing her interview with me? Well, we finished the interview and went to the pub to get something to drink. Once we were there Drew came in and joined us. I knew you were upset, but we didn't have a clue where you were. Drew said you borrowed his car and had errands to run. When I called you back it went to voice mail.

Drew sat on the arm of Tamara's chair and started gently rubbing her back. When he leaned close to her ear and again asked her if she was hurting any place, Tamara snapped back, "I've told you I'm all right, so don't ask again." After the words came out of her mouth she regretted them and immediately took Drew's hand and apologized.

"I didn't mean to say it that way. I know you're trying to help but I can't believe two people are dead. As much as I hated Pastor Hanson for what he did to me I didn't want him dead. All I know is that everywhere I go there seems to be trouble. Look at all the craziness I've caused here. And that poor undercover policeman, he's dead because he was investigating my case."

Stephanie's phone rang again and this time her whole demeanor changed. They knew she was speaking to Chief Parker because she kept saying, "Yes Chief, I know Chief, Okay Chief; I'll make sure it happens Chief."

She looked at Tamara and said, "That was the chief and he has changed the plans. He wants me to take you to the station to be interviewed. Apparently, Stedman was telling the officer this convoluted story about how you shot the pastor and then shot Erickson when he came into the office."

"That's crazy, I could never shoot at anyone. He was the one shooting at me."

"Let me finish. The Chief wants you at the station for two reasons. First, since Stedman made the accusation about you he wants the case to follow procedure and most witnesses in a murder case are interviewed in the station house. Secondly, the officer at the hospital stepped out of the room to call the chief and Stedman took the opportunity to run. So the chief wants you there for your own safety."

Drew said, "I'm going with you Tamara."

Stephanie added, "You're welcome to go to the station but I have to be the one taking her in. You can drive your own car. That way you'll have a ride when she's ready to leave." In reality, the police station was only a block and a half away from Drew's apartment and under normal circumstances would have been an easy walk. However, Drew still had a walking cast on and occasionally required a crutch, so it was far easier to drive.

Kathy turned to Stephanie and said, "It's still relatively early. Why don't you come back here after you're finished at the station? We can resume our talk." Kathy was giving a clear message to Tamara that she no longer was number one. If it hurt Tamara no one could tell because her composure stayed the same.

Driving to the station Stephanie asked Tamara, "How long have you two been together?"

"About three years, but it looks like that's all over now. Kathy already told me she was hooking up with other women at the shoe conventions and other business meetings. My falling for Drew shouldn't have come as too big a surprise. I told her when we first met that I was still attracted to men, and she said, "Wait till we've been together and you'll forget about men. I guess any break up is painful, and I love Kathy. She helped me through some real difficult times, but now I'm in difficult times again and she isn't able to help."

"Why do you say that?"

"Ever since we moved here together I've been the target of the hate groups, not Kathy. She convinced me that my parents wouldn't accept us as a couple and that her parents did. Then I find out her parents didn't support my relationship with their daughter and even attended Hanson's church on occasion. She never took my harassment seriously and even though I told her to stay in Chicago after our house was set on fire. I always thought she would come running to comfort me. The greatest hurt was her not showing up for the school board hearing. I think that put the last nail in the coffin."

As she pulled into the parking lot Stephanie said, "Kathy is an attractive woman with a commanding presence, and she comes across as a woman with a greater appetite than others. Do you think it's possible to love someone but still have sex with other people, because I think she loves you?"

"I agree with your comment about her having a bigger appetite than me for sure, and the way she looked at you, you're her next meal." With that statement Tamara exited the car with an inner feeling of satisfaction and headed to the station.

Chapter 32

Chief Parker and a detective, he introduced as Banks, took Tamara into an interviewing room. The chief informed her that the interview would be recorded and then read the Miranda rights to her. She didn't think she had any reason to fear since she hadn't done anything wrong, but a little voice was saying to her, "Never talk with the police without an attorney present." She pushed this voice down and told the chief she was ready for the interview.

The chief told her to tell them everything she had done since leaving his office this morning and try to remember every detail. She started slowly and as she became comfortable the speed of her dialogue increased.

"I was standing outside the station with Drew and Kathy and we were getting ready to leave when I saw Detective Stedman leaving the police station. I knew he was responsible for a lot of the problems I'd been having particularly reporting that lie about me inviting boys to have sex in the locker room at Blue Water State. I just knew if I followed him I'd learn something that clears my name. Since my Willy's is so identifiable I told Drew it wasn't running well and asked him if I could borrow his rental car to do some errands. Fortunately, Drew had already planned to do some physical therapy exercises because it would have been a problem if he had wanted to accompany me."

"I followed Stedman to the sheriff's office and waited outside for him. It was well after five when he left the office. I gave him lots of space and then followed. It didn't take long for me to figure out where he was going. I parked on the same dirt road as I did the other night and cut across the field to the church. I entered through a door by the maintenance room and snuck across the sanctuary and got close to Pastor Hanson's office."

"Stedman and Pastor Hanson were talking really loud. Stedman was telling him that he saw the undercover police officer with you, chief, when we met this morning. He was convinced that he was a cop and wanted to stop everything. He blamed Pastor Hanson for pushing the lesbian thing too far and there were heated words spoken. Just then the undercover police officer came into the church and went to the office. I couldn't see what was going on but from the sounds of it Stedman was beating the officer."

"I got out my phone and in the darkened space where I was hiding pushed "1" on my speed dial which was Kathy's number. Kathy answered but she was at the pub with the FBI agent and the noise along, with my whispering, didn't allow her to hear. I stopped calling because the voices were getting angrier. The Pastor tried to stop Stedman from beating the officer and they talked about each of them having plenty of money. The pastor said they each had almost half a million and Stedman said, no, he had almost a million. Then I heard a gunshot followed by another one. I didn't have any idea who'd been shot so I ran out of the building."

"Stedman must've heard me because he fired a shot at me when I was running across the field. There was no way he was going to catch me on foot. I knew that. When I got to the car I realized that I had lost my phone running from the church and drove home without thinking where I should go. So then I rushed to the apartments, going first to Drew's, and when he wasn't home I ran to mine. After I called 911, all I could think about was running away as far and fast as I could. I threw things in a suitcase and then called Kathy again. This time I was able to tell her what happened."

"I was almost to the stairway when Stedman was just about to the top. He aimed his gun at me and just then Drew and the others came in the door. Drew yelled and started coming up the stairs. Stedman turned and was going to shoot him point-blank when I tackled him. We both tumbled down the stairs, right at FBI Agent Willis' feet. I was okay after the fall, but I guess Stedman broke his wrist. That's the story."

Both Chief Parker and Detective Banks cross-examined Tamara for the next 45 minutes. They went back over her story several times trying to find some discrepancies, or at least getting additional information they didn't have before. They were particularly dogged on whether she ever entered the church office, but Tamara kept to her story. They released her from the interview while cautioning her to stay in town. The chief, probably attempting to make her feel more comfortable, said that he didn't think Stedman would be going after her.
His rationale was that Stedman accused her of the murders as a way to buy time.
"What he really wants is the money and he must be headed for it."

When she went back to the lobby Drew was waiting for her. A quick glance around the room was all she needed to realize Kathy wasn't with him. Drew embraced her and gently led her to his car. On the way back to the apartments Drew said, "I would be much more comfortable if you would stay in my apartment until Stedman is caught. I know you want to stand on your own two feet but this is a very unusual circumstance. You can stay in the second bedroom just to prove I'm not offering it as a way of getting you into bed."

Drew then chuckled and said, "Although I have to admit having you in my bed sounds like a delicious idea."

"Thanks for the offer. I think I'll take you up on it. I know I don't want to be alone and staying in the same apartment as Kathy would be really uncomfortable. Remember, I'm not moving in permanently so you don't have to worry about that."

"Why would I ever worry about that?"

Chapter 33

Drew accompanied Tamara to her apartment and thoroughly checked the unit with her to be sure Stedman wasn't there. It was obvious that Kathy wasn't there, and since it was now late in the evening Tamara assumed she was with Stephanie. Drew waited while she got some things together when he heard her laughing. She had the bag that she packed earlier on the bed and was laughing about the contents. She told him that she must have been really terrified earlier because she packed six pairs of socks two pairs of pajamas and one pair of jeans. This time she could be more leisurely about packing and got all the items she needed. Of course, she was only going down the end of the hallway, and it wasn't very far to go in case she needed something. Drew did notice that she stopped and wrote a note to Kathy telling her where she would be staying.

When they entered Drew's apartment Tamara went directly to his room. She looked at him and said, "I know where I want to stay and it's in your bed. I'm not a game player. When I made love to you in the past it was my decision, and a decision that I didn't make lightly. I told Kathy that I wanted to be with you, so why hide it?' My note to her told her where she could find me if she needed to get in touch. Any questions?"

That night, in spite of the fears and anxieties brought on by the shootings, Drew and Tamara were at ease. There were no longer any secrets, nor fears or feelings of recrimination, and most of all, no guilt. Drew didn't feel guilty for loving Tamara and Tamara didn't feel guilty for loving Drew. As much as he loved Shelly, he knew it was time to move on, and Shelly would have wanted him to find another love.

The night would have been perfect if it weren't for the gun pressed against Drew's head. They both were awoken by a loud voice saying, "Wake up right now and talk to me." It took a few minutes, but both Drew and Tamara seemed to recover quickly. Tamara was very conscious that she was naked beneath the sheets and tried to keep it up around her neck. At first she thought it was Stedman and immediately thought her life was over, but the voice didn't sound the same. Drew reached up and snapped the bedside light on and they both knew what they were facing.

There, holding a revolver aimed at Tamara was Joe Hanson, eldest son of Pastor Hanson. There were tears running from his eyes and he started talking. "Why'd you kill my father? He wouldn't do anything to hurt you. He just wanted you to leave town. Now you're going to pay for your sinning ways."

"Wait, wait, wait Joe," said Drew. "Tamara didn't kill your father. I don't know where you heard that but it isn't true."

"That's right Joe," continued Tamara. "I was in the church when it happened but I was hiding outside the office. Detective Stedman shot both your father and another man who was an undercover police officer. You have to believe me. Don't you think I'd have been arrested if the chief thought I was guilty? As far as I know you haven't done anything wrong yet. Don't do anything foolish. Don't do something you'd regret the rest of your life."

To Find What Was Lost

Joe's hands were shaking, and it was easy to see how agitated he was. Tamara knew she had to keep him talking, or at least have him allow her to talk to him. So she continued, "Joe, I heard them talking about money. Your father said that they had almost a half million between them and Detective Stedman told your father that he had almost a million. That is when he shot your father. Believe me, Stedman shot you father for money. Did you know your father had that kind of money?"

They could see that Joe was trying to put the pieces together but he wasn't the brightest star in the sky. He answered by saying that his father never had that kind of money and that they were lying. Tamara had a mantra going in her head, *Keep him talking.*

"Joe, who told you I shot your father?"

"I heard it from someone at the hospital. They heard Howie tell the cop."

"Joe, did you hear that Detective Stedman ran away from the hospital and that the police are looking for him now?"

For the next half an hour Tamara and Drew switched asking him questions and trying hard to keep him talking. As long as he was talking he wasn't shooting. Whether they each sensed that he didn't want to shoot them was uncertain, but it was evident that they felt he was beginning to hear their side.

They never saw the next thing coming and they were both surprised. Out of nowhere someone slammed into Joe's backside, knocking him across the bed and on to the floor.

Drew, bad leg and all immediately jumped on Joe and he was pleased and glad to see Jimmy Hanson join him. With Joe under control Drew excused himself so that he could get some pants on. Tamara whispered to Drew, "It would kill a homophobe like Joe if we told everyone how close your Johnson was to his face." Drew looked at her and was amazed that at a time like this she would find something funny. Going back to their first encounter when she had called him a Lower Lake Virgin, Tamara always had a crazy sense of humor.

Tamara pulled the sheet off the bed and went into the bathroom to change. Drew slipped on some pants and dialed 911. Within minutes the police were in his apartment and after a short interview arrested Joe for trespassing. They found out that Joe had used Jimmy's keys to the apartment building that he needed for the jobs he was doing for Drew. The officer thought trespassing was enough to keep him contained until they could further review the case.

It was now after 4:00 in the morning and nobody thought they could go to sleep. Drew said he was going to make some coffee and invited Jimmy to stay and have some. Tamara decided she might as well go the whole way and threw a pound of bacon in the oven on a cookie sheet and started breaking eggs for her special omelet. By 4:45 they each had several slices of bacon, a farmer's omelet and whole wheat toast in front of them.

Jimmy explained how he was spending the night at his father's house and woke up when he heard a car door slam. He wondered who was outside his house at 2:00 in the morning. He got to the window just in time to see Joe drive off. He told them that Joe was in terrible shape all night. He would have uncontrollable bouts of tears and then go into an all-out rage. He shared that Joe never completed school and was always dependent on their father. He added that his being sent away to a military school probably turned out to be one of the best gifts my father could have given him.

"Jimmy, you'd never turn out like Joe," said Drew. "We've worked a lot together and I know the kind of person you are. You're intelligent and hardworking. You never bought into that crazy stuff your father was promoting, which tells me you have good judgment. How'd you know to come here?"

"I didn't know where Joe had gone. My first guess was the church. I thought he was going to where my father died as a way of comfort. When he wasn't there I just started driving. It was really a fluke that I found him here. I noticed his car parked in the street which I thought was funny. So I put two and two together and assumed he was after Tamara. Nobody answered when I banged on her door and by chance I thought to try your place. I could tell whenever I was around the two of you that something was going on so I rushed to your place. I'm glad I got here before anything bad happened."

As they were finishing up their breakfast there was a knock on the door and Chief Parker was standing there. Drew invited him in and said, "Chief, I didn't know your day started at 6:00"

"For some reason, Drew, ever since you got to town my days just haven't been the same."

Drew read the sparkle in his eye for what it was and said, "Has my mother got you all tied up in knots, because we can do something about that."

"That's another story; you know darn well what I'm talking about. House fires, bodily assaults, killings and now another attempted homicide are all part of your everyday existence. That isn't what we usually experience here in Manitou. Enough of this nonsense, I just wanted to check on you personally because when I get a call from out east I want to say that I personally saw that you were in good health."

He pulled a little note pad out of his pocket and said, "You might as well tell me what you know, and start at the beginning okay?" Drew looked at the man and thought how much respect he had for him. The guy seemed unflappable. He didn't down play anything and gave each issue his full attention. His next thought was that his mother could do a lot worse than Ed Parker.

The chief actually spent a fair amount of time with Jimmy asking questions about his father's financial situation. Jimmy was very honest with him and said that he spent the last few years away from home. His father never talked much about money at home, but there also wasn't a lack of it. Joe never worked outside the house and his father always made sure he had pocket money.
"I used to be jealous of Joe until I realized that his life was pretty sad. I know my father had him do some pretty bad things, but deep down I don't think Joe is a bad guy."

To Find What Was Lost

Chapter 34
The chief had a busy schedule planned for the day, and in a way he was thankful he got called in at 6:00 in the morning. His first call was to Col. Tom Powers of the Michigan State Police, and this was a very difficult call to make. Tom had lent him an officer and now that officer was dead. All law enforcement officers know that they face life or death each day but nobody wants it to happen on their watch. Tom was very supportive and told the chief he already had had several conversations with Josh's mother. The chief got her name and number so he could call her personally. He also got the details on the funeral so that Manitou Police could be represented at it. Fortunately, Josh did not have a family of his own yet but he did have parents and a fiancé and he took down their numbers so he could call them.

He interviewed Joe and almost felt guilty because Joe said he didn't want an attorney present and then began to incriminate himself. Joe admitted to being at the fire and providing the bales of hay. He also admitted to hitting Drew with a golf club. The Chief asked many questions about his threatening Drew and Tamara with a gun. Joe said, "That was just a pellet gun. My dad would never let me have a firearm as much as I begged him."

"Tell me again everything you did last night?"

"I couldn't sleep and kept wandering around the house. Jimmy went to bed after the Late Show but I stayed up. I kept thinking about that girl and how she ruined everything for me. My dad was sure that she was responsible for everything bad in the city and I believed him. He wanted her out of town and told me to scare her good. I made a mistake and got the bales of hay too close to the house, and the fire started burning the house. My dad was really mad at me for that, and he told me so. I saw Jimmy's keys in the jar by the door and knew he had keys to the apartments. So I got the key and drove to the apartments. I went to the big apartment and opened the door with Jimmy's keys. I found that Bathsheba in bed with Drew, and that's when I really lost it."

The Chief asked, "What did you want to do to them?"

"I don't know. I wanted them to hurt like I hurt. I liked seeing them scared but when they started talking I got confused. They both said that Howie Stedman shot my dad. At first, I didn't believe them but when she talked about hearing Howie tell my father he had all the money it made me think. My dad had me leave the room several times when he was meeting with Howie. He always said they had money business to talk about and I wouldn't understand it. My dad always took care of me and now that he is dead I don't know what to do"

"I'll tell you what I'm going to do," said the Chief. "I'm going to arrest you on several charges including arson, physical assault and battery, trespassing and assault while using a weapon. You're going to be placed in the county jail and the judge will assign a public defender to handle your case. The things you've done are bad Joe and you more than likely will be sentenced to some jail time. How you handle yourself from this point on is very important. Please cooperate with my officers and follow the directions at the jail. You will be taken care of in jail. "

To Find What Was Lost

There was little doubt in Chief Parker's mind that Joe has some significant cognitive limitation and that his father used Joe's big size by making him his strong arm. He was glad that he recorded the whole interview and that he was careful about interviewing without an attorney present. At this time jail would be a safe place to keep Joe but the chief worried about what would happen to him if he were sent to prison.

Jimmy Hanson was at the police station completing his report of the incident. When he saw the chief he asked for a minute. "Chief, Joe is not all there, you know what I mean. He was easily led by our father and always used his strength to get things done. I can't tell you how many times Joe whopped me because my father told him to do it. But that being said, he is not a bad person. He can have a really kind streak. I know he was really confused last night, but he wouldn't have hurt Drew or Tamara."

"Jimmy, I have placed Joe under arrest and will make sure that he has an attorney. But he admitted to assaulting Drew and that assault almost was murder. He also set the house on fire. So you can't convince me that he wouldn't hurt someone because he already has hurt someone."

"Chief, I have to believe that our father was the cause of all that and without him Joe will do much better. Anyway, that's all I've got to say. I know you're busy, but thanks for listening."

When the chief got back to the office there was a message to call the Michigan State Police Crime Lab. They had put a special rush on their investigation because it was one of their own. The chief got right through to the forensic specialist and learned that the murders were staged to look like they shot each other. When they did all the measurement and used lasers to trace the entry and exit of the bullets it was clear they didn't kill each other. Furthermore, he said, "If I had to guess Officer Erickson was shot first at close range. We initially could only account for four of the five shots fired, but we did find a shell casing at the outside door of the maintenance area and assume that was the shot fired at Ms. Elwell."

He went on to tell the chief they examined the clothing collected from Detective Stedman when he was at the hospital and found significant traces of gunpowder blowback on his shirt sleeves. He obviously had shot a weapon in recent time.

The chief checked on the APB that had been put out on Howard Stedman stating that he was wanted for questioning after leaving the custody of a police officer. The chief told his administrative assistant to change the APB to state that he was wanted for a double homicide and should be considered armed and dangerous. He poured himself a cup of coffee and closed his office door. After sitting for a second he picked up his phone and dialed a familiar number. When the phone was answered, he reclined in his chair and said, "How's your day going?"

Barbara Ashley was surprised to hear from Ed in the morning. They usually talked at night so she assumed something was up. "I'm good Ed; you must have something to talk about since you called this early?"

To Find What Was Lost

"Well, yes, I have something to talk with you about, but more importantly I needed to hear your voice. It has a real calming effect on me and believe me I need it. First, there has been another incident involving Drew and Tamara but they are both all right. I tell you Barb, we've talked about the two of them having a thing for each other. I can tell you it is for real. Tonight, or this morning at around 3:00 our officer was called to Drew's apartment where both were interviewed in their pajamas. I don't think they were having a pajama party either."

She chuckled and responded, "What happened?"

They talked for over a half an hour, and the chief filled her in on everything that had happened including the murders. The only thing that he could use to give her hope was that with Pastor Hanson deceased and Stedman on the run, the attacks on Tamara would stop. They ended their conversation the same way they had for the past several weeks. Bye, I miss you and love you.

Chapter 35

For some reason the sky seemed a little bluer and the air fresher. Fall in Michigan is a great time of the year and Tamara was enjoying the day. She should have been tired after losing so much sleep but instead she was wide awake. Drew was off at physical therapy and Tamara was sitting on the rooftop deck drinking another cup of coffee and watching the gulls ride the off shore breeze.

She heard someone climb onto the deck and at first thought it was Drew. When she turned to look it was Kathy. "You really should keep your door locked you know," said Kathy.

"I'm feeling so safe now and I know it's silly, but just having Pastor Hanson and Stedman gone is like a breath of fresh air. I didn't want either the pastor or the undercover cop to die and almost feel guilty that I'm feeling so good about the pastor's death. It was horrible yesterday in the church. I could hear the gunshots and knew that people were dying. I have never been in a situation like that before and never want to be again."

"I'm the one who feels guilty," said Kathy. "Everything you said about me is true except that I do love you. I'm afraid that isn't enough for me. When I get away I can't help but see an attractive woman and wonder if I can get her in bed. It hurt when you accused me of seducing you when you were most vulnerable. At first I was furious that you said it that way, but then I did an honesty check and had to agree with you. It's strange to say you love someone but then want to cheat on them with the first warm-blooded female you meet. Please forgive me, but I think I have the morals of a rabbit."

With that acknowledgement, something changed in their relationship. Tamara laughed and said, "That's very descriptive and probably accurate judging from the way you were licking your chops looking at Stephanie. Kath, it's been a lovely ride, but it's over and we both know it. I love what you've meant to me and only wish you the best but I'm certain that my heart is with Drew."

They sat for the next hour talking about everything that had happened. Tamara filled her in on all the details including the phone call she received from Chief Parker telling her they were charging Stedman with murder and that Joe Hanson was under arrest for a number of charges. They were just getting ready to leave when Drew stuck his head through the deck entryway. He pulled himself up and proudly announced that he now only had to wear a lightweight brace and could start putting pressure on the leg.

They all decided to go to the pub that evening like old times. Tamara asked Kathy if she wanted to invite Stephanie, but Kathy said she'd already left for Indianapolis with lots of records she collected from Pastor Hanson's office. The pub was full of the usual assortment of locals and it was obvious they all wanted to hear the details from Tamara, Drew and Kathy. Finally, Drew stood up and announced in a loud voice. "We'd love to tell you everything, but the chief has told us we have to be quiet or he can put us under arrest."

When he sat down Tamara said to him, "That's not true Drew". He responded, "I know but look how it quieted the peanut gallery." Suddenly, the fourth chair was pulled out from the table and Addie joined them. The four of them looked at each other and no one said it but they all felt like it was old times. The rest of the night was a blast. The pub had Karaoke Night and they all had a chance at the mike. The room really cracked up when Drew took the mike and announced he was doing a song he loved to sing in "Glausta". That started it when the crowd started yelling, "Where's that place? What did you say?" Drew looking so serious said, "You know 'Glausta', the greatest and oldest seaport in America."

The next morning came too quickly. Tamara wanted to get a run in since her schedule had been really screwed up. Drew said he had some business to take care of in Traverse City and would be back in the afternoon. The meeting with the school board was happening in two days and there was something he needed to do. He had searched the internet and found that an Ed Conover was track coach at a small college in Alma Michigan. Checking his GPS he learned that Alma was a little under three hours from Manitou so he left as soon as Tamara went for her run.

Although it felt great to just have a brace on his leg, Drew could feel the muscles cramping throughout the ride. The steel rod was still in the leg and may be there for a long time. But he didn't know if that was bothering him and assumed it was muscles being used for the first time in weeks. The trees were starting to turn and he realized that Vermont isn't the only place with beautiful fall scenery. The rolling hills of Michigan covered with a variety of hardwoods made a beautiful patchwork quilt of colors.

His GPS system directed him to the house listed as belonging to Edward Conover. It was a small ranch with bikes, balls, and a hockey net on the side of the driveway telling everyone that children lived there. He knocked on the door and waited as he heard someone moving inside. The woman who opened the door could have been called attractive if her hair was groomed and she wasn't in baggy, soiled sweats. She was probably in her late thirties or early forties. As he looked at her, he realized she looked really tired. Her skin was blotchy, and her eyes red. She was hand brushing her uncombed hair when she saw Drew.

"Hi, my name's Drew Ashley and I'm looking for an Ed Conover who was the assistant coach at Blue Water State about 8 to 10 years ago. Is this his house?"

"Yes," she wearily replied. "But Ed's not here. What do you want with him?"

"When do you think he'll be back because I really need to speak with him?"

"Mr. Ashley, Ed won't be back. He died about 4 months ago."

Just then Drew felt like any chance of correcting the lie told about Tamara at Blue Water State had been taken away. Evidently, Mrs. Conover noticed his distress and asked if he needed a glass of water or something. When he said yes, she invited him in. The house looked well lived in, and most of the furnishings were old and worn.

After handing him a glass of water she talked, "Please pardon the way the house looks. To be honest since Ed's death I have had trouble getting motivated."

"If you don't mind my asking, how did he die?"

"In February, he was diagnosed with pancreatic cancer and by June he was dead. It was fast moving but I'm sure for Ed it wasn't fast enough. He sure suffered in those four months. I took a leave of absence from my job at the bank and haven't been able to go back since."

Drew was thinking how he could ask this woman if her husband had had an affair with a student at Blue Water State. Then he thought another way around it would be to ask about the rape. "I am trying to assist a friend of mine who may lose her teaching job. Some parents filed a phony complaint of morals charges which she was able to win, but then a man came into the hearing and said that she willingly had sex with two members of the track team in the equipment room. She denied it and said she was forcefully raped. She said your husband saw it happening and then refused to help her. Did Ed ever talk about an incident of rape? Her name is Tamara Elwell. Perhaps you remember her name?"

She gasped as if the air was sucked out of the room and Drew didn't know if she was going to faint and or flee the room. So he asked her if she was all right because it was clear to him that she wasn't.

"All I can think is that God is punishing me and I don't know why."

Drew chose to remain quiet and it worked because she continued, "Our family has never been very religious. I mean our kids were baptized and we go to church on Easter and Christmas but that was about it. When Ed was first diagnosed with cancer he thought he could beat it. When chemo did nothing and the doctors told him he had less than 6 months Ed started going to church. It was just a small Methodist Church in town, but the minister was about his age and spent hours talking with Ed. One of the things they talked about was leaving this world with a clear conscience."

"About a month before Ed died the Minister was visiting and asked me to join them. At first I thought it was going to be a prayer session or something. When I entered the room the Minister said that Ed had to tell me some things he did that have been weighing on his mind. With that the Minister left the house and Ed started talking."

"It's so strange that you come here and mention Tamara's name. Sure I knew Tamara. She was a superstar and also one of the kids who were always at the house. The thing weighing on Ed's mind was Tamara. He started crying as he told me that he had had an affair with Tamara. I was shocked and cancer or not I felt like leaving him right then to suffer alone. What he said next really knocked me off my feet. He told me that he broke it off with Tamara but she wouldn't leave him alone. She threatened to tell me and his way of handling that was to encourage two male runners to rape Tamara. Then he told Tamara if she talked to anyone about their affair he would go on record as saying that she seduced the boys."
"Why he had to tell me that before he died just to clear his own conscience was beyond me. I thought we always had a wonderful marriage, but after hearing what he did I felt so emotionally abused. The Minister came back regularly until Ed died and tried to tell me how important it was for Ed to leave this world with that off his chest. What he did was destroy me and I'm left trying to hold the family together.

The kids can't understand what's happened to me and I can't ruin their memory of their father and tell them the truth."

Drew stood and walked over to her. Putting his hand on her shoulder he said, "It was a long shot coming to see if I could convince Ed to talk to the board. Tamara has been through more than you can imagine, and to lose her teaching job on moral grounds will crush her. Thank you for listening to me anyway. I am sorry for your loss."

As he was walking to the door he stopped and turned, "I have to tell you something. About two years ago my wife reminded me that I needed to pick up a birthday gift for my mother since she was coming to dinner that evening. I told her I was busy and she took our son and left the house to get the gift. I heard a crash and got to the bottom of my street just in time to see my wife and son engulfed in flames. I stopped living for a year and became someone my wife wouldn't recognize. It wasn't until my wife's mother made a special trip to visit me and basically kicked me in the ass. She told me to crawl out of the hole, stop the pity party and get back to living. I'm telling you that you cannot let his deathbed confession define you or your relationship with your husband. You have too much to live for, and your kids must really be missing their mom when they need her the most."

Two people were absorbed in their own thoughts. Paige Conover was thinking about everything that man just said to her. She was mad that he accused her of being in a hole and not meeting her kids' needs. Then she burst into tears with the realization that everything he said was true. She had stopped living, mad over an affair Ed had a number of years ago and disappointed that he wasn't the man she always put on a pedestal.

On the way home Drew made all the right turns according to his GPS, but his mind was somewhere else. It had been some time since he remembered all his feelings about losing Shelly and he was surprised how fast they came back. It was different now in that the sad memories were only part of his life with Shelly and he could recall at will the wonderful life he had had with her. He soon shifted his thoughts to Tamara. Any plan to get the school board to reject the morals charge seemed to be squashed. All he wanted to do was get home to her. Whatever happened at the school board they could handle it together.

Chapter 36

Chief Parker had everything wrapped up in the murder case except catching the murderer. FBI Agent Willis called him to report that she identified eight people who had turned over their estates as well as their deeds to their homes to Pastor Hanson. On the up side, Pastor Hanson wasn't a really smart thief and left lots of documents unprotected. One of the documents talked about a non-profit set up in Aruba called Christians Serving Christians. Using the resources of the FBI, she learned that it was a dummy corporation and not serving any purpose other than serving its two officers, Pastor Ralph Hanson and Howard Stedman.

She also said that two of the people leaving money to the pastor had died within a couple of weeks of signing the papers. Neither of these individuals had any family so there was no one checking on them or questioning the cause of their deaths. She said her supervisor was particularly pleased because she found corroborating information in his files about the frauds he committed in Indiana. She told Chief Parker that she only regretted his death because she would have loved seeing this man locked up for life.

They talked about Howie Stedman and agreed that he was going to try to get the money in Aruba. She sent out notices to all international airports in the United States with flights to Aruba alerting them to be on the lookout for Howard Stedman. She added in her alert that he probably had a broken arm or wrist. Within a day she called the chief to report that he had been arrested trying to board a plane at the Gerald R. Ford Airport in Grand Rapids. He had a ticket to fly to Aruba non-stop. Since murder was the greater of the two crimes and he was arrested in Michigan he was transferred to the Manitou County Jail to await his trial on first degree murder. The Feds said they would wait to try him on fraud charges.

Drew and Tamara were both at home when Chief Parker knocked on Drew's door. After a quick hello he said that Kathy told him they'd both be there. The Chief said that he wanted to tell them in person that Howie Stedman had been arrested and was currently on his way to the county jail awaiting arraignment. Although neither Drew nor Tamara thought that Stedman was a threat to them now, it was comforting to know he was arrested.

The chief added that he planned to attend the school board meeting tomorrow and to testify as to the character of both Pastor Hanson and Detective Stedman. He didn't know if it'd do any good but it certainly couldn't hurt.
Tamara was truly appreciative of his gesture because it showed faith in her. Even with the chief coming she already made up her mind that they'd release her. Just this week alone was enough to cause them to be wary of her. Here she was on paid leave and still involved in a double murder. She was already thinking about other jobs. Working at Silent Sports didn't seem like a plan since it would put her and Kathy together so much.

After the chief left Drew said, "Let's do something different to get your mind off the school meeting. Do you have anything you'd like to do?"

"You know what; there is something I'd like to do. When I was in middle school I was quite a dancer. Two summers I went to Interlochen Arts Academy and studied dance. I had the greatest time and learned so much there. You may not believe it but things I learned about body movement at Interlochen made me a better runner. By ninth grade the track coach had my summers all planned, and dancing wasn't part of it."

"The campus is less than an hour from here and I'd like to visit it for old time's sake. We can grab something to eat at one of the local places and then attend the student dance performance in the evening."

Dancing wasn't Drew's thing but he wasn't going to say that to Tamara. "Let's go. It sounds like a great day."

Riding in a car is a perfect time to have an uninterrupted discussion and that was just what occurred. Maybe it was facing a grieving widow or maybe it was just time but Drew told Tamara about his relationship with Shelly. He started at the beginning and told her what first attracted him. He told her about some of their wilder dates. He told her about how he proposed and all about the wedding. He shared how he felt when Bobby was born and talked about the first house they bought together. Finally, he talked about losing her and the guilt he carried as a result of her death. He unloaded a ton of burden and for the first time in a couple of years felt totally free.

The visit to Interlochen was inspiring. The year-round residential arts academy was something totally new to Drew. There were practice rooms and small studios all over the campus. The kids who weren't in class or taking lessons were like any other teenager, texting, laughing, and a few were even playing Frisbee. After a nice dinner in a little German restaurant in town they were back in time for the dance performance. Corson auditorium looked like something you'd find in a big city and was a great venue for dance. The highlight of the evening was the dancing, and although all of it was beautiful, Drew really liked the tap.

Maybe Tamara was thinking about how open and honest he had been on the ride up. As difficult as it was for him to share some of the personal details Tamara never felt closer to him. She knew it was her turn. He knew a good amount of her life before college so she started talking about her freshman year. She talked about some of the boys she dated and how much time cross-country and track took up. She shared how important coaches become to students and then she took a leap of faith and told him everything about Coach Conover.

Tamara said that he was an attractive guy with boyish good looks. All the girls liked him and flirting with him was an everyday occurrence. Then she started struggling with her words as if they were new to her. She told Drew that in her mind she seduced him. Whereas the other girls openly flirted, she was coy. When she knew he was near the locker room she'd find ways to accidently flash him. He invited the team to his house on many weekends and his wife was really sweet. However, the first time they kissed was at his house with his wife in the next room.

She shared how their affair rapidly progressed from there and they were always looking for a place to meet and make love. She really believed he'd leave his wife and when she told him that he was shocked. He thought they were just hooking up and told her he'd never leave his wife. She was embarrassed telling him how she'd threatened to tell his wife and thinking back on it couldn't believe her behavior. However, it was talking about the rape that brought out the most painful memories. She said the rape was over quickly. It was two young guys and they came almost immediately. They didn't hit her or anything like that. One held her down while the other penetrated her and then they switched places. What really hurt was when she found out the coach set it up as a way to prevent her from talking to his wife.

They arrived home about 10:00 p.m., and both were emotionally drained. When they finally were in bed Drew put his arm around her waist and she snuggled into him. They slept like that all night and when they awoke in the morning they were in the same position. It was almost as if being intimate would have interfered with the bond they had formed that day.

Chapter 37

When her cell phone rang at 9:00 Tamara had just woken up. The other side of the bed was empty and had been for a while since it was cool to her touch. Her mother was on the other end of the line and asked if the school board hearing was still on for tonight. She told Tamara that they were on their way to Manitou and would be there late afternoon. Of course, Tamara told them they didn't have to come to the hearing but they wouldn't hear of it. They arranged to meet for dinner at a local restaurant and then would go to the meeting together. Tamara said, "I'll bring Drew along too if that's all right?" Her parents were more than pleased to have Drew join them for dinner.

When Tamara finally got to the kitchen she found a note from Drew. It said the coffee was on and he had picked up scones from Jimmy's Juice & Java this morning. He added that Kathy wanted to talk with him so he was in her shop if she needed him. Tamara just assumed they were meeting about some landlord business and didn't think about it again.

She had just finished her 2nd cup of coffee when the house phone rang. It was Barbara Ashley, Drew's mother, Tamara explained that Drew wasn't there and Barbara told her she really had called to talk with her. Barbara explained that she wanted Tamara to know that she would be thinking of her today. She also expressed her great concern about the murders and the fact that Tamara could have been injured. It was apparent that Barbara had been filled in by Chief Parker because she knew all the details. After several minutes they ended their conversation and Tamara realized there were lots of people in her corner.

The early dinner with her parents was very positive and really kept Tamara's mind off the hearing. What made it very special was that her whole family was there. Her brothers, John and Austin, made the trip to give her moral support. John had to fly from Philadelphia where he is in grad school so she was very surprised to see him. There was lots of family talk, and if Drew felt out of place it wasn't noticeable. He fit so comfortably in the family she didn't think at all about him as an outsider. Driving to the school board meeting Drew told her how much he liked her family. He shared that he feels like he missed out a lot being an only child with a single mother.

The school parking lot was packed an hour before the meeting. Now instead of just the local TV stations they had all the national networks there. Lots of familiar television reporters were lined up in front of the school hoping to talk with anybody close to the case. Of course, the double homicide that had occurred during the week only increased the media attention. This story now involved rape, a lesbian love affair, a radical fundamentalist preacher, a corrupt police officer, fraud and a double murder. It fed the prurient interests of America's TV viewing population that was fascinated by reality shows and at this time they weren't even aware of Tamara's sexual relationship with her coach.

The temptation for five minutes of fame was too great for some people and many were jousting in front of the cameras hoping they'd be on TV. Tamara and Drew were hustled into the building but couldn't help but see some of the girl's track team being interviewed as well as the mayor. One could only wonder how information they possessed could add to the story. When they got to the auditorium it was already full and someone had gone to the trouble of setting up large screen TV's in the gym and cafeteria for the overflow crowd. Drew thought if they sold tickets the school could probably have funded a couple of new academic programs.

Tamara, Drew and the Elwell family were sitting in the front row. Tamara noticed that Kathy and the Muellers, her parents, were sitting on the opposite side of the auditorium 10 to 15 rows back. Unlike last week, there were no protestors outside or inside the building. This audience seemed to be there because it was the best show in town. When the school board and superintendent entered from the side stage the audience became very quiet.

The President of the school board banged his gavel on the podium and said in a formal way, "May we stand for the pledge of allegiance." Once everyone was seated he began, "This special meeting of the Manitou Board of Education is called to order. The purpose of this meeting is to share with Tamara Elwell the board's decision regarding the charges made against her. We are aware of the horrible tragedy of the murder of Reverend Hanson and the Michigan State Police Officer and our thoughts are with their families at this time. We also recognize that Howard Stedman, a key witness, is in jail and not available for further questioning. Nevertheless the board had already made its decision before those events and do not think they change the outcome voted upon. Therefore, Tamara Elwell, as president of the board it is my duty to tell you ----.

"Stop," a woman's voice yelled from the back of the auditorium. She ran down the aisle with a teen age boy following closely behind. It took Drew a second to recognize

Paige Conover because her appearance was so drastically different. The change from yesterday was dramatic because today she appeared to be a very attractive woman who had it all together. Tamara also recognized her and grabbed Drew's arm whispering, "That's Paige, the coach's wife. What's she doing here?" When she got to the front of the auditorium she spoke.

"May I please speak? My name is Paige Conover and I have something very important to say that is critical to the outcome of this matter. The President was somewhat taken off guard by this woman and said, "You have three minutes to address the board."

"My name is Paige Conover and my husband was an Assistant Coach at Blue Water State University during the time that Tamara Elwell was a student. I knew Tamara as a great athlete and good student. Until very recently that's all I knew about her. I am sad to say that my husband lost a very brief battle with cancer and died four months ago. Shortly before his death, a minister who had been helping him deal with end of life issues suggested that he clear his conscience of some very bad things he had done." She started to get choked up and the Superintendent brought her a glass of water.

"What he told me was shocking and so unlike my husband that it put me into a severe depression. For the past four months I haven't worked, been a recluse and barely have been able to care for my children. It wasn't until Mr. Ashley visited me two days ago that I realized my husband's confession was destroying my life." She turned and nodded her head to Drew. Tamara leaned over and asked why he didn't tell her, all the while knowing he wouldn't answer at that time.

"My husband was a good man and a wonderful father but he told me he did something terrible while coaching at State. He said he'd had an affair with a student and led her on to the point that she thought he was going to marry her. When she had a hard time over the breakup and threatened to tell me about the affair, he arranged to have two male students drag her into the equipment room and rape her. He then told her if she told anyone about their affair he would call on the boys to report how she seduced them."

"Ed never could forgive himself for what he did and I didn't think I could continue to live knowing about it. I just heard about this hearing from Mr. Ashley and the report that some detective gave last week making it appear that Tamara was immoral. After Mr. Ashley left my house I felt great relief sharing what Ed had told me. Basically, Mr. Ashley told me to crawl out of the hole I was in and stop the pity party. He said that I couldn't let his deathbed confession define me or my memories of my husband. I realized that Ed would have wanted me to right this wrong and that's why I am here tonight."

She looked directly at Tamara and said, "I'm so sorry for everything you've been through." Getting through this confession in front of a huge audience became too much and she burst into tears. Her son took her arm and started to lead her toward the back of the auditorium, but before she took too many steps Tamara took her hand and led her to empty seats in the front row.

Paige Conover wasn't the only interruption of the meeting because shortly after she sat down another group entered the auditorium. The entire track and cross-country teams dressed in their uniforms, both male and female, walked down the aisle. When they got to the stage the captains of the teams stepped forward and each spoke to the board. The speeches weren't necessarily eloquent but they were heartfelt. They were high school kids trying to express to the board how important Coach Elwell was to them, and everyone in the auditorium felt their sincerity. One of the Captains made a point of saying that every member of both teams were present to support Coach. This statement was significant because at the last hearing there were parents of kids on the team obviously against Coach Elwell.

They thanked the board for listening to them and then turned and walked toward Tamara. Each player stopped and either shook her hand or hugged her depending on their own comfort level. Tamara was standing to greet the players and there were plenty of tears flowing and not just on Tamara's cheeks.

The President of the board stated that since this is a personnel matter and the meeting is closed to the public, the board was going to a classroom for a brief meeting. After the two unexpected presentations by Paige Conover and the student teams the teary eyed audience was emotionally worn out. What occurred was not what most of them thought would happen that night. Most of the people in attendance expected Tamara to be fired even though the vast majority was on her side.

The board returned in less than 15 minutes and the President stood up and made one quick statement. "Ladies and gentlemen, the Manitou School Board has considered the charges brought against Tamara Elwell and unanimously find that they are not credible. This matter is considered over and Tamara Elwell is welcomed back to her teaching and coaching positions. The Board apologizes for any undue pain this hearing may have caused her." It was over that quickly and the auditorium burst out in cheers and applause.

Tamara turned to Paige and said, "Paige, I can't tell you how much I appreciate what you did tonight. I can only begin to understand how difficult it had to be for you. I also offer my condolences to you and the children. It had to be such a difficult time for you and then to endure Ed's confession. Please believe me when I say I personally regret my actions and only hope that you realize I was just a naïve student. I'd never have wanted you or Ed to suffer the kind of pain and sorrow that you've been going through.

Paige thanked her for her comments and they hugged the way casual acquaintances hug at weddings and funerals. It was clear they weren't going to become best buds, but a huge crossroad had been passed for both of them. Paige was finally in a position to move on with her life, and Tamara got the acknowledgment that she had been victimized as a student. It wasn't a perfect resolution but it was a resolution they both could accept.

Drew stepped forward and asked Paige if she and her son needed a place to stay for the night. It was after eight and they would have a three hour ride ahead of them. Paige thanked them but explained, "That's why I brought Bud along to help with the driving. I have to get back to the younger children. They really need me right now," and looking directly at Drew she added. "I've started to dig myself out of that hole so I'm ready for them."

It took Tamara over 45 minutes to get out of the school. Everybody wanted to talk with her and she felt a need to recognize those who came out in support of her. When she reached the sidewalk the media was still there. Drew told her he could get her away from them but Tamara stopped him. "I'm done running from things that scare me. I want to talk to them."

Drew decided that the best way to handle it was like a press conference and to tell the media present that she would entertain some questions. So Drew corralled the national media and everyone else followed. It took a little while to get control of the group, but then it proceeded like any other news interview. What Drew quickly realized was that Tamara had a message she wanted to get out. She repeated the same message in different ways several times. The message she kept repeating was that same sex couples are no different from heterosexual couples other than the legal definition. She said for her it was about love and she doesn't define herself as being lesbian, straight or bisexual. She said she is just a human being who has a great deal of love to give and responds equally to someone who loves her.

There were some questions about her love affair with a coach and her involvement in the double murder of Pastor Hanson and State Trooper Erickson that she answered in brief responses. There were also some questions about her cross-country and track team as well as her past achievements in running. The final question took her by surprise when a local TV reporter from Traverse City said, "Rumor has it that you have separated from your partner and are now living with a man. Is that true?" Tamara thought for a minute, looked at Drew, and then answered, "Remember I said it's about love, that's what is important in any relationship. I can tell you that yes, I am in love, and you can figure out the rest."

It was too cold for the deck so Drew suggested that everyone meet at the pub for a drink and some food. The Elwell's, Tamara and Drew found that the pub was packed but two groups invited them to join their tables. Soon the tables were pushed together and everybody found some place to sit around it. It was difficult to tell if the celebratory feeling was because of the hearing results, but whatever the circumstance, the place was hopping. Tamara sat with her parents and Drew observed that they often touched each other and occasionally spoke but there was no denying the sense of connection. Tamara looked radiant and indeed she was the star attraction.

By 11:30 they all were drained and exited the pub together. The Elwell's were staying at a local motel and arranged to meet with Tamara and Drew for breakfast. Drew and Tammy walked hand in hand to the apartment, Before Drew opened the door he looked at her and said, "Did you mean what you said tonight? You know, about being in love.".

Tamara said, "I meant every word I said. Why, is there something you didn't understand?"

"I wanted to be sure that you'll take good care of my heart, because I'm giving it to you. I love you, Tamara, and being with you makes me the happiest man in the world."

Their mood reflected the way they were both feeling. It was a sense of freedom from all the things that held them back before. They had cleared away the rotten memories and experiences that messed up current day activities.. They were free and able to express their love in so many ways.

To Find What Was Lost

Chapter 38

The next morning while getting ready to eat breakfast with her parents, Tamara realized she hadn't turned her phone back on since before the meeting. She was shocked to see there were over 45 messages for her. She started pressing to listen to them and then deleting the messages as they were from every newspaper, radio and television network around. A couple of times she was shocked to know that some really big name talk show stars wanted her on their show. The phone started ringing while she was listening to messages, so she thought the best thing to do was shut it off again.

They met at the locals favorite breakfast place and were pleased to get seating right away. The restaurant had made a name for itself because it served big breakfasts, but most of the customers this morning looked like tourists up for the color tours. While waiting for their breakfast to arrive they heard Manitou being mentioned on the TV. The Today show hosts were talking about the school board hearing and how Tamara's interview after the hearing had gone viral. Tamara looked around but didn't see any of the other customers looking at the TV. If it had been locals there they would have turned immediately when the name Manitou was mentioned.

During breakfast Tamara told her parents how many messages she had on her phone and that they ranged from a local radio station to the most famous lesbian talk show host on TV. She was hot right now and they all wanted a piece of her. They knew that their audiences would eat up stories about her and thus their ratings would increase. High ratings meant they could charge more for advertising. It was all sort of a vicious circle. Tamara said, "I really don't want to be on

TV or write a book or have a movie made about my life. I want this all to go away and let me live my own life."

Carl Elwell spoke up and said, "You realize, Tamara that won't keep someone else from writing a book and capitalizing on your story. You should think it through more carefully before you say no."

"Okay Dad, I'll keep an open mind on the matter." This was her way of appeasing the analytical side of her father. He was notorious for checking everything several times before he made a decision. Tamara remembered his comprehensive studying of all makes of washing machines before he selected the "right" brand. He even did this when picking a location for their summer vacation. Everyone in her family was used to it and usually told him what he wanted to hear, whether they did it or not.

After saying their goodbyes Drew and Tamara were heading back to the apartment when Tamara asked him to pull over. She quickly jumped out of the car and proceeded to vomit. As soon as she finished she got back in the car and said, "That came on fast. I can't believe it was anything at breakfast. Maybe it was all the pressure from the hearing, and I did drink and eat too much at the pub last night. Oh well, I feel good enough right now."

Before they reached the apartment Drew's cell phone rang. He pulled over again and answered. He looked at Tamara as he was talking and told the caller that she was with him. He then said that they could meet right now if that worked and ended the call with a quick goodbye.

To Find What Was Lost

"That was Kathy on the phone. She wants to meet with the two of us and assumed we would be together."

"Did she say what she wants?"

"No, she just said it was important that we meet today."

They arrived at Silent Sports and Kathy led them back to the office. She looked at Tamara and said, "I am so happy that things turned out at the hearing. I just couldn't be there for you at the first hearing and I regret my actions but that's how it is. Last night, sitting with my parents during the hearing, made me realize how far they still had to go before they truly accept me. But this isn't the reason why I needed to meet."

"Ultimate Shoes has been trying to get me to join their team. They finally came up with the big number. I will be the Manufacturer's Rep for everything east of the Mississippi. This means I'll be on the road constantly and cannot manage the store. This is a huge opportunity for me personally. I'd be working for one of the finest running shoe companies in the world, and it'd also get me away from Manitou. I need to be away from my parents and you. You'll probably agree that it'd be good for you if I weren't a tenant of Drew's too."

"What are your plans for Silent Sports? You've two more years on the lease and both you and Tamara are co-owners. Do you plan to hire a manager while you're on the road?"

"I guess what I'm saying is that I want out anyway I can get there. If that means I sell my part of the partnership fine. I actually was thinking that Tamara was going to lose her job and be able to take over the whole shop. That's why I haven't talked about this before today."

"I'm in a state of shock Kathy," said Tamara. "We were partners in this venture and I would've thought that you would have warned me of your plans. However, I'm in even greater shock that you thought I'd be fired. You've been running the business and taking your salary out of it. To support the store I haven't taken any money out of the business but as a result I left everything up to you. I have no idea of the inventory, ordering, or for that matter the financials. I'm embarrassed to say I trusted you completely with running the store since you were being paid as the manager."

"All right, "said Drew. "Let's focus on what we need to know for now. Kathy is leaving and she wants to sell her portion of the business. So the questions are simple. When do you plan to leave, and what value do you place on your half of the business?"

"I told Ultimate Shoes I could be onboard November 1st. I've done some figuring and I believe my part of the business is worth $150,000."

"Kathy, that means you will be gone in a few weeks. How could you make such a commitment without talking to us?"

Throughout this discussion Drew was trying to be a problem solver. He knew that Kathy's actions were also meant to hurt Tamara and it was clear she was hurt. At the same time he was thinking through the business end of the deal. Unless Kathy could show him on paper that half the business was worth $150,000 he wouldn't believe it. She wasn't selling the whole business and selling half of it wasn't worth as much as selling the whole thing.

He asked Tamara what her thoughts were about the business. She looked at both of them and said she planned to stay in teaching and coaching. She wasn't planning on running the business and if it helped the sale she would sell her half too. Tamara had said that, from the beginning, the business was Kathy's baby and she invested in it to show her support of Kathy.

Drew took over and thanked Kathy for sharing with them. He said that Tamara had some big decisions to make and he recommended that they take the rest of the day to think about it. In the meantime he asked Kathy if he could look at the books and also talk with her accountant. She realized that if she was going to sell the business reviewing her books was going to be part of it.

Drew immediately called the accountant and set up a meeting for both Tamara and him in the afternoon. He then took the books to the apartment and started reviewing them. Overall he was surprised how well the business was doing and when he told Tamara that Kathy was taking almost $90,000 in salary plus health insurance she was blown away. The business was far more successful than most of the shops along the downtown strip. One of the real moneymakers was the shoe contracts she had with all the high school athletic teams and the factories. This was like picking money off the proverbial money tree in the backyard.

Early next morning Tamara was up ready for a run. She was surprised to see Drew come out dressed in his running clothes. This was the first day that he could try running again and he wanted to start a gentle jog with her. After less than a mile he had to stop and that allowed her to finish the run in her usual fashion.

As they were taking an easy jog along the river walk Drew asked Tamara what she wanted to do with the store. He told her that it was a successful business and could easily support her and a few part-time employees. She reaffirmed what she said yesterday, that her commitment was to teach and coach. Besides she said, "I don't have money to buy out Kathy."
They reached the mile point and Drew stopped, ready to walk back home. "You did great for your first time back, honey. Is the leg hurting?"

"I definitely know that it was broken. I probably will have the rods removed in the future but we'll see. I do have to ask you something important. What would you think if I bought Kathy's half of Silent Sports? I've studied the financials and met with the accountant, and Kathy wasn't far off in the valuation. If you're not comfortable with me as a partner, I'm prepared to buy your half too."

"Wow, this changes everything. Let me finish my run and we'll talk when I get home."

Her use of the word home wasn't lost on him, but he didn't know what she was thinking about being his partner. He stood for a moment to watch her graceful stride down the river walk and had the same feelings as the day he met her months ago. All of a sudden she stopped and leaned over. He couldn't tell if anything was wrong, but after a minute or so she continued on her run.

To Find What Was Lost

Back at the apartment Drew had sketched out a plan to present to Tamara. In studying the books he quickly found a couple of places that he could significantly grow the business. The challenge would be convincing Tamara that it'd work. After she came out of the shower and was dressed for school he presented his plan. "Tamara, I think Silent Sports can grow, and here are the areas I'd like to focus on."
"Drew, there isn't enough space to add those lines."

"There is if we buy the store next to us and open the wall between them. I know you'll say you don't have the money but you don't need it. I'll do the total investment and I know you won't be comfortable unless you are paying for it. So what'll happen is your share of the ownership will decrease to one-third from one-half. I'll absorb all the cost of acquiring the building and buying additional inventory. If things go as I expect your one-third of the new and improved Silent Sports will be worth 2 to 3 times what your one-half was worth. All I want to hear you say is that you'll be my partner."

Her kiss on his lips sealed the deal.

Chapter 39

By the first week in November Drew was the owner of Silent Sports with Tamara Elwell as his partner. He was as excited as a child with a new toy. He had owned the car wash business but that wasn't very satisfying. Most of his employees were on probation and the customers were some of the biggest complainers around. It was totally different in this new business. He felt like he was really helping people in Silent Sports. They wanted what he had to sell and when he met their needs they were thrilled.

It took some wheeling and dealing to get the owner of the building next to him to sell. Drew had Mike Edwards, now his close friend, inspect the entire building. Mike had a list of major problems that would be facing the current owner in the future. Still, the owner was only lukewarm about selling the building. There was a small insurance agency leasing the store which also had to be dealt with. Drew had to offer a bit more than it was worth, but in the end the deal was done. Mike started on the renovation immediately and Drew got Addie's help in relocating the insurance agency to a better space for less money

The building needed a lot of work and Mike had drawn up extensive plans. One of the bigger challenges was having the face of the newly acquired building match the Silent Sports.. The interesting thing was that the second floor was totally unoccupied. At one point in its history it had been an Odd Fellows' Hall, so there were four very large rooms. One of the rooms was for their ceremonies, one was for their social gatherings, one was their dining room and the last was a commercial kitchen. The rooms hadn't been touched in over fifty years, and it was like stepping back in time. Overall, there was about 3,500 square feet, which was a very large space for downtown.

The building plans looked really good to Drew until one day he went up on his deck and looked over to the adjoining roof. It was a flat roof, but in pretty bad shape. What interested Drew the most was that it could accommodate a nice sized deck. So he asked Mike to check on the structure to be sure it could hold the deck and then, unlike in his current apartment, Drew wanted a full set of stairs leading to the roof.

Jimmy was on the job with Mike, and Drew noticed he had been promoted from a "gofer" to a framer. One day during lunch Drew asked Jimmy how Joe was doing. Jimmy reported that he was still in jail and his hearing was coming up in a couple of months. The court-appointed attorney thought that he would get at least two years for the assault that caused bodily damage. Jimmy said that Joe doesn't really understand why he's there because in his mind he was doing what his father wanted done.

The newspaper reported that Howard Stedman's trial wouldn't be till the spring. Tamara had already been notified by the Prosecuting Attorney that she would be called upon as a witness. It looked like an open and shut case. Probably the only thing saving Stedman from the electric chair was that Michigan doesn't have the death penalty. The FBI had done an excellent job investigating the fraud and located a good portion of the money. An independent financial manager was appointed to distribute the money back to the victims.

Tamara was interested in the new store and how it was going to connect with the existing shop. Drew showed her the upstairs, and she got a real kick out of seeing how things must have looked decades ago. He told her they were going to put a few apartments up there when Mike got the chance.

About the second week in November Drew got a call from his mother saying she was coming for Thanksgiving. He had to kid her a bit and tell her she probably didn't want to see him at all. She bit on his joke and told him he was right so could he make room at the Thanksgiving table for Ed and two of his daughters. Now, out of the blue, he was hosting Thanksgiving. When he mentioned it to Tamara she got all excited and said she wanted to invite her family too. Drew tried to count how many were coming, but lost count on his fingers.

Chapter 40

 The day before Thanksgiving Drew was standing at the window of Silent Sports when a rental truck drove up. At first he thought it was a delivery for the shop, but then he saw a familiar face getting out of the passenger side. It was Bess Currier his mother's next door neighbor from Gloucester and then around the front of his truck came his mother. *What the hell*, thought Drew as he hurried out to greet her? "What are you doing in this truck, Mum? Oops, hello there Bess, sorry to ignore you."

"This truck has all the belongings I care about. I'm here for good. I got to thinking why do I have to stay in Gloucester? The people I really want to be with are in Michigan. So I sold the house and most of my belongings. Everything I own is in this truck and to tell you the truth the whole experience is personally renewing. I haven't felt so alive in years. I didn't want to drive out here alone, and Bess told me she would love the adventure. So here I am. You don't suppose you can put me up in your spare bedroom till I find a place on my own?"

"I can do better than that. Tamara and Kathy's apartment is unoccupied at the moment, and you can use it till you find a place. Heck, Bess can stay here as long as she wants to," teased Drew.

Just then they heard a siren and saw police lights flashing. Next, they heard a voice over the megaphone say, "You can't park there lady. Move it along." Barbara turned and ran to the cop car getting there just as Ed was climbing out. He grabbed her and their kiss even embarrassed Drew. Bess chuckled and told him that all she'd heard about for 700 miles was Ed, Ed, Ed.

Drew enlisted the aid of Jimmy Hanson and they rented two eight-foot tables and fifteen folding chairs for the Thanksgiving dinner. He was busy all afternoon running errands for Tamara, but it was for the best. Tamara, his mother and Bess had taken over the kitchen and were having a great time making pies, rolls, appetizers and anything that could be made in advance. Drew's chores involved getting plastic tablecloths, napkins, wine, beer, and soft drinks. He also was told that one of the turkeys would be grilled up on the deck and that was also his job.

Thanksgiving Day started out like a typical late November day in northern Michigan. The sky was a brilliant blue, but you could see your breath every time you blew out. The women were up and in the kitchen before Drew climbed out of bed. He had read all about grilling the turkey and set about preparing it. First, he had to rub down the turkey with peanut oil, then cove the wings with foil and last but not least get the coals white-hot and over to each side for indirect cooking. Before he left to fire up the grill Drew put his arms around Tamara and whispered to her "Are you ready?" She replied, "Ready, willing and able."

Around 2:00 p.m., Drew's house was full of activity. Tamara's parents Carl and Pat arrived along with her two younger brothers John and Austin. Chief Parker got there about the same time with his two daughters Cindy and Sue. His oldest daughter is married and lives in another part of the state. Barbara Ashley's old neighbor from Massachusetts, Bess, had been in the kitchen for hours helping Tamara. Earlier in the week Drew had also invited Jimmy Hanson since was really alone now.

There were a lot of introductions made because almost nobody knew everybody. The mix of ages was great for assigning tables. There were 5 people who were in their late teens and early twenties. The second table Drew and Tamara being the youngest, so it allowed them to sit with their parents. They had been eating appetizers since about 12 o'clock, and most of them didn't have a clue how they would be able to eat everything on the table. If you thought of every kind of traditional Thanksgiving food, it was all on their table.

Just before they started, Drew stood up and announced he wanted to offer a toast. He'd bought champagne for the occasion and made sure there was a glass in front of everyone. Just when he was going to say, "let's raise our glasses", Austin, Tamara's brother, hollered out," Tamara only has water." Drew ignored him and said, "I'll begin again. This has been an amazing year for Tamara and me in every way possible, ranging from the worst to the best. We've talked a lot about it and one thing that makes it special is all the new friends we have. To have both our families and our friends gathered here warms our hearts. It is for that reason that we want you to know…."

Drew didn't finish before Tamara stood up and interrupted him saying, "We're going to have a baby." The table erupted with cheers. Both mothers rushed to Tamara and hugged her. Carl Elwell shook Drew's hand and everyone was joyous. Barbara, who doesn't hold back anything, said, "Okay, when are you two getting married?"

Drew answered, "Don't rush us just yet. We just found out about the baby this week. Believe us, it wasn't planned but I think I can speak for Tamara in saying we are both overjoyed."

The meal was fantastic and the desserts out of this world. As they neared the end of the meal Drew stood up again and said, "The women worked awfully hard to put on this meal. I suggest we send them to the living room and the men clean up from dinner. Once we're done there I'd love to show you what we've been doing in the building next door."

The women cheered but then Tamara said, "As much as I appreciate your gesture honey, I'm afraid of what the kitchen will look like when you're done. You won't know what to put where. What you can do is clear the table and wash the pots, pans and serving dishes. How's that?"

After clean-up, the whole group toured Silent Sports and Drew told them about the new products he was introducing into the shop, including kayaks, city bikes, skate boards, roller blades and ice skates. The opening in the wall between Silent Sports and the other building was complete as was most of the work. He then led them outside to the entrance and stairway leading to the second floor. When they reached the top everyone looked around in wonder. The drywalls were up and the wood floors installed, but nothing was painted. The ceilings were 18 feet high and made the space seem immense.

Drew explained that when he saw this space it was too good to pass up, so he turned it into a single apartment for his

To Find What Was Lost

family with three bedrooms, a study, three bathrooms, living room, family room and kitchen.

Tamara looked at him and said, "No wonder you kept telling me Mike was dragging on finishing the apartments."

Drew smiled and said to everyone, "I'd like to show you a really special place. Follow me." He led them up a beautiful staircase that opened to the rooftop deck.

The deck was covered with rose petals except for a small table holding a tiny box. Drew picked up the box and got down on one knee. When he opened it there was a huge solitaire diamond surrounded by many tiny diamonds. He held the ring up to Tamara and said, "Tamara you'll make me the happiest man on the earth if you will marry me."

Before she could answer a lower laker blew its horn notifying the draw bridge tender that it was coming up the channel. Tamara pulled Drew up into her arms and said, "I guess you're not a lower laker virgin any more, are you? By the way the answer is yes."

The End

Made in the USA
Lexington, KY
30 September 2018